LONGMAN IMPRINT BOOKS

A James Joyce Selection

A selection of his early prose and poetry with a sequence
of photographs showing James Joyce's Dublin

edited and introduced by
Richard Adams
Lord Williams's School, Thame

Longman

LONGMAN GROUP LIMITED
London
*Associated companies, branches and representatives
throughout the world*

This edition first published by Longman Group Ltd
in association with Jonathan Cape Ltd 1977

Dubliners, A Portrait of the Artist as a Young Man
and **Chamber Music** are published by Jonathan Cape Ltd
Extracts from these books are included in this volume
by arrangement.

Editorial and supporting material in this Longman
Imprint Books *edition* © Longman Group Ltd 1977.

ISBN 0 582 23355 0

We are grateful to the Society of Authors for permission to
reproduce the following copyright material: 'A Flower Given to
My Daughter', 'On the Beach at Fontana' and 'Ecce Puer' by
James Joyce. Reproduced by permission of the Society of
Authors as the literary representative of the Estate of James
Joyce.

We are grateful to the following for permission to reproduce
photographs: Mansell Collection, page 122; National Library of
Ireland, pages 109, 111, 112–13, 116–17, 118, 119, 120, 123, title
page and cover; Radio Times Hulton Picture Library, pages 110,
114, 115 and 121.

Companion cassettes, with readings of some of the key stories are
available for the following titles in the series:

The Leaping Lad and other stories
The Human Element
A Sillitoe Selection
Late Night on Watling Street
A Casual Acquaintance
Loves, Hopes, and Fears
A John Wain Selection

Printed in Hong Kong by Shek Wah Tong Printing Press Ltd.

iv

A James Joyce Selection

Longman Imprint Books
General Editor: Michael Marland

Titles in the series

*THIS EDITION IS FOR
DAVE AND FLIP*

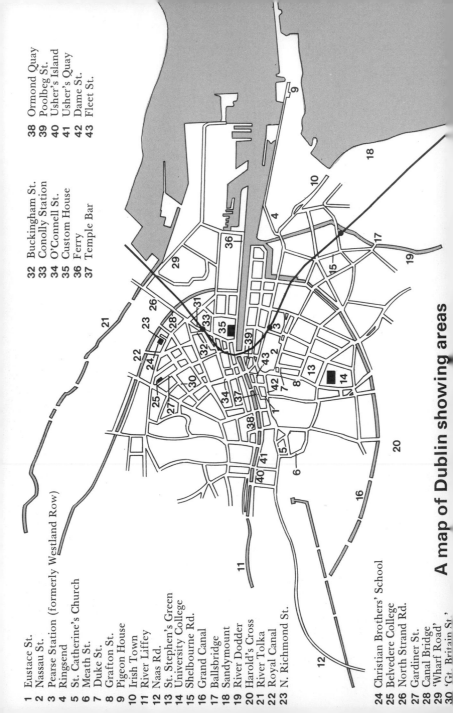

A map of Dublin showing areas

1 Eustace St.
2 Nassau St.
3 Pearse Station (formerly Westland Row)
4 Ringsend
5 St. Catherine's Church
6 Meath St.
7 Duke St.
8 Grafton St.
9 Pigeon House
10 Irish Town
11 River Liffey
12 Naas Rd.
13 St. Stephen's Green
14 University College
15 Shelbourne Rd.
16 Grand Canal
17 Ballsbridge
18 Sandymount
19 River Dodder
20 Harold's Cross
21 River Tolka
22 Royal Canal
23 N. Richmond St.

24 Christian Brothers' School
25 Belvedere College
26 North Strand Rd.
27 Gardiner St.
28 Canal Bridge
29 'Wharf Road'
30 'Gt. Britain St.'

32 Buckingham St.
33 Conolly Station
34 O'Connell St.
35 Custom House
36 Ferry
37 Temple Bar

38 Ormond Quay
39 Poolbeg St.
40 Usher's Island
41 Usher's Quay
42 Dame St.
43 Fleet St.

Contents

Introduction

People's attitudes, ways of life, and the structure of our society have changed since the time before the First World War when most of these pieces were written, but as James Joyce based them on his own life and real experience they are still interesting and relevant to us today. The ways of the world may change, but the inner feelings of life remain the same and are vividly brought to life in Joyce's writings.

These pieces are grouped into four sections:

Finding Out includes stories about the growth of awareness and experience of life of a small boy;

Loves and Conflicts leads naturally from this, and deals with the joy as well as the problems of falling in love, perhaps for the first time;

Parents deals with various aspects of the relationship between children and their parents; and finally,

On Our Own takes us into the world of adult responsibility.

Most of the episodes that have been chosen are set in Dublin, the city where Joyce grew up and lived for many years. As we read through *Dubliners* and *A Portrait of the Artist as a Young Man*, a clear picture of the place slowly emerges before our eyes: the shops, streets, houses, schools, offices, rivers, pubs. These are the background against which he sets the people and events of his stories, and, as I have already pointed out, many of these people and events are drawn from life. But even when he was not recalling actual men and women or actual situations, Joyce still used his own experience of life to make his writing ring true. His characters are the *sort* of people who lived around him as he grew up, and they are the *sort* of people who exist today. They are real in the sense that they are believable, and this too is why they appeal to us over half a century later. In a similar way, Joyce's situations and events are likely and interesting from our point of view because at the very least they are the sort of situations and events which were going on around him all the time. He creates nothing that is impossible or sensational for its own sake.

James Joyce

James Joyce was born in Dublin on 2 February 1882, the eldest of a family of ten children. His father, John, was a civil servant, at one time employed in the office of the Collector-General of Rates and Taxes in Dublin. He had come originally from Cork, where, at the time of James's birth, he still owned several properties. He was a vivacious, witty, talented man, but he also had a tendency to spend more freely than he could afford and to drink too much. The result was that between James's birth and the time of his first travels on the continent at the age of twenty, the family, as its fortunes declined, was obliged to move through a depressing succession of more than a dozen small and increasingly shabby houses. In spite of the instability of his father's financial position, however, James received a sound education, first at Clongowes Wood College and later at Belvedere College. Many of his experiences during his school years are recorded in both *Dubliners* and *A Portrait of the Artist as a Young Man*: the encounter with the strange man while playing truant with his brother, Stanislaus; the pandying; the trip to Cork with his father; the incident on the night of the Whitsuntide play. In these books too he preserved portraits of many of the people with whom he came into contact day by day. The names are changed, but in the characters that live in the pages of *Dubliners* and *A Portrait of the Artist as a Young Man*, we are in fact catching glimpses of the author's family, acquaintances and friends. You can get some idea of the Dublin of that time from the sequence of photographs beginning on page 109.

James was a hardworking student, and at the relatively early age of sixteen he gained admission to University College, Dublin, where he studied modern languages. It was during his time at university that he began to make a serious start on his career as a writer, producing poetry, reviews, magazine articles and plays. In 1902 he left Dublin for Paris. It was the first of many journeys about Europe with which his life was to be punctuated. He began to move in international literary circles, and to be recognised as an important newcomer. After a brief return visit to Ireland in 1903–4, during which time he wrote parts of *A Portrait of the Artist as a Young Man* and some of the *Dubliners* stories, he set off on his travels once again. With him on this occasion went a young woman called Nora Barnacle. They had two children, even though they did not marry until 1931.

In the years that followed, Joyce spent most of his time travelling the continent with Nora, working on his two most celebrated books, *Ulysses* and *Finnegan's Wake*, fighting the prejudice with which his writings were greeted, and struggling to have them published. In 1917 he contracted a severe eye disorder, which plagued him for the rest of his life. But this, and the operations he was forced to undergo as a result of it, did not prevent his continued pursuit of his literary career and his determination to explain, through what he wrote, something of himself, of the world in which he grew up, and of their impact on each other. He died in Zürich, Switzerland, on 13 January 1941, at the age of fifty-eight.

Any facts about Dublin or his life that you need to know to follow the writing are explained briefly at the foot of the relevant page. Other background information and points that you will find help your understanding of each piece are grouped in the section 'More about the Writing' (page 125).

Your Own Writing

Joyce's creative technique – the method, that is, by which he bases his writing on his knowledge and experience of life – is one we would do well to imitate. The surest way of making our writing honest and interesting to others is not by inventing unlikely people or events just to create sensational effects, but by filling it with our own firsthand observations. One of the principal aims of this book is to help you, by focusing your attention on your own experiences, to write stories, anecdotes, poems or compositions – all of which have the ring of authenticity and truth. In the section headed 'Thoughts and Developments' (page 131) you will find a variety of questions about characters and situations which appear in the passages from Joyce's books. You are invited to put forward your own opinions, to recount your own experiences, to express your own feelings. You might take some of these questions as the basis for a class or group discussion, or you might simply use them as aids for thinking out your own ideas alone. At all events, they should lead to some form of writing and you will find suggestions and topics appended to each group of questions. These suggestions are very general and open-ended. They aim to give you plenty of scope in your treatment of themes: you may be inclined to write a purely descriptive passage, or it may turn out to be a story; you may write as if you are the chief character involved in the action, or you may write as if it is all happening to someone else, perhaps an entirely imaginary person; you may set your writing in the present, or it may take place in the past. All these things are possible so long as you write honestly and accurately, and try to describe people, events and background as they really are in life. If you want precise help in working on one of these topics for writing, then you may go back to the extract itself. As you prepare your own ideas, ask yourself these questions:

1 Has this ever happened to me?
2 Has a similar situation ever arisen involving me?
3 Is it a likely situation? Has it ever happened to anyone I know?

4 What was it like? How would I have felt? What emotions did I experience – fear? hope? affection? hatred? jealousy? panic? horror? How would I have reacted? What might it have been like if things had been slightly different?

5 What were the precise circumstances and surroundings of the events – time of year? weather? what time of day? place? other people present? How carefully and precisely can I create the background to my story?

6 How were my senses involved – touch? taste? smell? sight? hearing?

7 Above all, how can I make sure that what I remember or can imagine clearly is conveyed just as clearly to my readers?

If you bear this sort of detail in mind, you will find that even the most commonplace experiences take on a new life and a new interest for other people, and that ordinary day-to-day events will acquire for you an added richness and significance.

R. A.

Finding Out

1
The Sisters

There was no hope for him this time: it was the third stroke. Night after night I had passed the house (it was vacation time) and studied the lighted square of window: and night after night I had found it lighted in the same way, faintly and evenly. If he was dead, I thought, I would see the reflection of candles on the darkened blind for I knew that two candles must be set at the head of a corpse. He had often said to me: 'I am not long for this world,' and I had thought his words idle. Now I knew they were true. Every night as I gazed up at the window I said softly to myself the word paralysis. It had always sounded strangely in my ears, like the word gnomon[1] in the Euclid and the word simony[2] in the Catechism. But now it sounded to me like the name of some maleficent and sinful being. It filled me with fear, and yet I longed to be nearer to it and to look upon its deadly work.

Old Cotter was sitting at the fire, smoking, when I came downstairs to supper. While my aunt was ladling out my stirabout[3] he said, as if returning to some former remark of his:

'No, I wouldn't say he was exactly . . . but there was something queer . . . there was something uncanny about him. I'll tell you my opinion. . . .'

He began to puff at his pipe, no doubt arranging his opinion in his mind. Tiresome old fool! When we knew him first he used to be rather interesting, talking of faints and worms; but I soon grew tired of him and his endless stories about the distillery.

'I have my own theory about it,' he said. 'I think it was one of those . . . peculiar cases . . . But it's hard to say . . .'

He began to puff again at his pipe without giving us his theory. My uncle saw me staring and said to me:

'Well, so your old friend is gone, you'll be sorry to hear.'

'Who?' said I.

[1] a geometrical figure described by the ancient Greek mathematician Euclid
[2] the illegal practice of buying or selling promotions in the church
[3] porridge

'Father Flynn.'

'Is he dead?'

'Mr Cotter here has just told us. He was passing by the house.'

I knew that I was under observation so I continued eating as if the news had not interested me. My uncle explained to old Cotter.

'The youngster and he were great friends. The old chap taught him a great deal, mind you; and they say he had a great wish for him.'

'God have mercy on his soul,' said my aunt piously.

Old Cotter looked at me for a while. I felt that his little beady black eyes were examining me but I would not satisfy him by looking up from my plate. He returned to his pipe and finally spat rudely into the grate.

'I wouldn't like children of mine,' he said, 'to have too much to say to a man like that.'

'How do you mean, Mr Cotter?' asked my aunt.

'What I mean is,' said old Cotter, 'it's bad for children. My idea is: let a young lad run about and play with young lads of his own age and not be . . . Am I right, Jack?'

'That's my principle, too,' said my uncle. 'Let him learn to box his corner. That's what I'm always saying to that Rosicrucian there: take exercise. Why, when I was a nipper every morning of my life I had a cold bath, winter and summer. And that's what stands to me now. Education is all very fine and large . . . Mr Cotter might take a pick of that leg of mutton,' he added to my aunt.

'No, no, not for me,' said old Cotter.

My aunt brought the dish from the safe and put it on the table.

'But why do you think it's not good for children, Mr Cotter?' she asked.

'It's bad for children,' said old Cotter, 'because their minds are so impressionable. When children see things like that, you know, it has an effect. . . .'

I crammed my mouth with stirabout for fear I might give utterance to my anger. Tiresome old red-nosed imbecile!

It was late when I fell asleep. Though I was angry with old Cotter for alluding to me as a child, I puzzled my head to extract meaning from his unfinished sentences. In the dark of my room I imagined that I saw again the heavy grey face of the paralytic. I drew the blankets over my head and tried to think of

Christmas. But the grey face still followed me. It murmured; and I understood that it desired to confess something. I felt my soul receding into some pleasant and vicious region; and there again I found it waiting for me. It began to confess to me in a murmuring voice and I wondered why it smiled continually and why the lips were so moist with spittle. But then I remembered that it had died of paralysis and I felt that I too was smiling feebly, as if to absolve the simoniac[1] of his sin.

The next morning after breakfast I went down to look at the little house in Great Britain street. It was an unassuming shop, registered under the vague name of *Drapery*. The drapery consisted mainly of children's bootees and umbrellas; and on ordinary days a notice used to hang in the window, saying: *Umbrellas Re-covered*. No notice was visible now for the shutters were up. A crape bouquet was tied to the door-knocker with ribbon. Two poor women and a telegram boy were reading the card pinned on the crape. I also approached and read:

July 1st, 1895
The Rev. James Flynn (formerly of S. Catherine's Church, Meath Street), aged sixty-five years.
R.I.P.

The reading of the card persuaded me that he was dead and I was disturbed to find myself at check. Had he not been dead I would have gone into the little dark room behind the shop to find him sitting in his arm-chair by the fire, nearly smothered in his great-coat. Perhaps my aunt would have given me a packet of High Toast for him and this present would have roused him from his stupefied doze. It was always I who emptied the packet into his black snuff-box for his hands trembled too much to allow him to do this without spilling half the snuff about the floor. Even as he raised his large trembling hand to his nose little clouds of smoke dribbled through his fingers over the front of his coat. It may have been these constant showers of snuff which gave his ancient priestly garments their green faded look, for the red handkerchief, blackened, as it always was, with the snuff-stains of a week, with which he tried to brush away the fallen grains, was quite inefficacious.

I wished to go in and look at him but I had not the courage to

[1] someone who practises simony, which is the sin of selling church positions

knock. I walked away slowly along the sunny side of the street, reading all the theatrical advertisements in the shop-windows as I went. I found it strange that neither I nor the day seemed in a mourning mood and I felt even annoyed at discovering in myself a sensation of freedom as if I had been freed from something by his death. I wondered at this for, as my uncle had said the night before, he had taught me a great deal. He had studied in the Irish college in Rome and he had taught me to pronounce Latin properly. He had told me stories about the catacombs[1] and about Napoleon Bonaparte, and he had explained to me the meaning of the different ceremonies of the Mass and of the different vestments worn by the priest. Sometimes he had amused himself by putting difficult questions to me, asking me what one should do in certain circumstances or whether such and such sins were mortal or venial[2] or only imperfections. His questions showed me how complex and mysterious were certain institutions of the Church which I had always regarded as the simplest acts. The duties of the priest towards the Eucharist and towards the secrecy of the confessional seemed so grave to me that I wondered how anybody had ever found in himself the courage to undertake them; and I was not surprised when he told me that the fathers of the Church had written books as thick as the *Post Office Directory* and as closely printed as the law notices in the newspaper, elucidating all these intricate questions. Often when I thought of this I could make no answer or only a very foolish and halting one upon which he used to smile and nod his head twice or thrice. Sometimes he used to put me through the responses of the Mass which he had made me learn by heart; and, as I pattered, he used to smile pensively and nod his head, now and then pushing huge pinches of snuff up each nostril alternately. When he smiled he used to uncover his big discoloured teeth and let his tongue lie upon his lower lip – a habit which had made me feel uneasy in the beginning of our acquaintance before I knew him well.

As I walked along in the sun I remembered old Cotter's words and tried to remember what had happened afterwards in the dream. I remembered that I had noticed long velvet curtains and a swinging lamp of antique fashion. I felt that I had been

---

[1] the early Christian burial places in Rome

[2] a sin which could be pardoned, as opposed to a mortal (deadly) one, which could not

very far away, in some land where the customs were strange – in Persia, I thought . . . But I could not remember the end of the dream.

In the evening my aunt took me with her to visit the house of mourning. It was after sunset; but the window-panes of the houses that looked to the west reflected the tawny gold of a great bank of clouds. Nannie received us in the hall; and, as it would have been unseemly to have shouted at her, my aunt shook hands with her for all. The old woman pointed upwards interrogatively and, on my aunt's nodding, proceeded to toil up the narrow staircase before us, her bowed head being scarcely above the level of the banister-rail. At the first landing she stopped and beckoned us forwards encouragingly toward the open door of the dead-room. My aunt went in and the old woman, seeing that I hesitated to enter, began to beckon to me again repeatedly with her hand.

I went in on tiptoe. The room through the lace end of the blind was suffused with dusky golden light amid which the candles looked like pale thin flames. He had been coffined. Nannie gave the lead and we three knelt down at the foot of the bed. I pretended to pray but I could not gather my thoughts because the old woman's muttering distracted me. I noticed how clumsily her skirt was hooked at the back and how the heels of her cloth boots were trodden down all to one side. The fancy came to me that the old priest was smiling as he lay there in his coffin.

But no. When we rose and went up to the head of the bed I saw that he was not smiling. There he lay, solemn and copious, vested as for the altar, his large hands loosely retaining a chalice. His face was very truculent, grey and massive, with black cavernous nostrils and circled by a scanty white fur. There was a heavy odour in the room – the flowers.

We crossed ourselves and came away. In the little room downstairs we found Eliza seated in his arm-chair in state. I groped my way towards my usual chair in the corner while Nannie went to the sideboard and brought out a decanter of sherry and some wine-glasses. She set these on the table and invited us to take a little glass of wine. Then, at her sister's bidding, she filled out the sherry into the glasses and passed them to us. She pressed me to take some cream crackers also, but I declined because I thought I would make too much noise eating them. She seemed to be somewhat disappointed at my refusal and went over quietly to the sofa, where she sat down behind her sister. No one spoke: we all gazed at the empty fireplace.

My aunt waited until Eliza sighed and then said:

'Ah, well, he's gone to a better world.'

Eliza sighed again and bowed her head in assent. My aunt fingered the stem of her wine-glass before sipping a little.

'Did he . . . peacefully?' she asked.

'Oh, quite peacefully, ma'am,' said Eliza. 'You couldn't tell when the breath went out of him. He had a beautiful death, God be praised.'

'And everything . . . ?'

'Father O'Rourke was in with him a Tuesday and anointed[1] him and prepared him and all.'

'He knew then?'

'He was quite resigned.'

'He looks quite resigned,' said my aunt.

'That's what the woman we had in to wash him said. She said he just looked as if he was alseep, he looked that peaceful and resigned. No one would think he'd make such a beautiful corpse.'

'Yes, indeed,' said my aunt.

She sipped a little more from her glass and said:

'Well, Miss Flynn, at any rate it must be a great comfort for you to know that you did all you could for him. You were both very kind to him, I must say.'

Eliza smoothed her dress over her knees.

'Ah, poor James!' she said. 'God knows we done all we could, as poor as we are – we wouldn't see him want anything while he was in it.'

Nannie had leaned her her head against the sofa pillow and seemed about to fall asleep.

'There's poor Nannie,' said Eliza, looking at her, 'she's wore out. All the work we had, she and me, getting in the woman to wash him and then laying him out and then the coffin and then arranging about the Mass in the chapel. Only for Father O'Rourke I don't know what we'd done at all. It was him brought us all them flowers and them two candlesticks out of the chapel and wrote out the notice for the *Freeman's General*[2] and took charge of all the papers for the cemetery and poor James's insurance.'

---

[1] anointed with consecrated oil by a priest as a preparation for death

[2] Eliza means the *Freeman's Journal*, a Dublin newspaper

'Wasn't that good of him?' said my aunt.

Eliza closed her eyes and shook her head slowly.

'Ah, there's no friends like the old friends,' she said, 'when all is said and done, no friends that a body can trust.'

'Indeed, that's true,' said my aunt. 'And I'm sure now that he's gone to his eternal reward he won't forget you and all your kindness to him.'

'Ah, poor James!' said Eliza. 'He was no great trouble to us. You wouldn't hear him in the house any more than now. Still, I know he's gone and all to that. . . .'

'It's when it's all over that you'll miss him,' said my aunt.

'I know that,' said Eliza. 'I won't be bringing him in his cup of beef-tea any more, nor you, ma'am, sending him his snuff. Ah, poor James!'

She stopped, as if she were communing with the past and then said shrewdly:

'Mind you, I noticed there was something queer coming over him latterly. Whenever I'd bring in his soup to him there I'd find him with his breviary[1] fallen to the floor, lying back in the chair and his mouth open.'

She laid a finger against her nose and frowned: then she continued:

'But still and all he kept on saying that before the summer was over he'd go out for a drive one fine day just to see the old house again where we were all born down in Irishtown, and take me and Nannie with him. If we could only get one of them new-fangled carriages that makes no noise that Father O'Rourke told him about, them with the rheumatic wheels, for the day cheap – he said, at Johnny Rush's over the way there and drive out the three of us together of a Sunday evening. He had his mind set on that . . . Poor James!'

'The Lord have mercy on his soul!' said my aunt.

Eliza took out her handkerchief and wiped her eyes with it. Then she put it back again in her pocket and gazed into the empty grate for some time without speaking.

'He was too scrupulous always,' she said. 'The duties of the priesthood was too much for him. And then his life was, you might say, crossed.'

[1] book containing the services of the Roman Catholic Church

'Yes,' said my aunt. 'He was a disappointed man. You could see that.'

A silence took possession of the little room and, under cover of it, I approached the table and tasted my sherry and then returned quietly to my chair in the corner. Eliza seemed to have fallen into a deep reverie. We waited respectfully for her to break the silence: and after a long pause she said slowly:

'It was that chalice he broke . . . That was the beginning of it. Of course, they say it was all right, that it contained nothing, I mean. But still . . . They say it was the boy's fault. But poor James was so nervous, God be merciful to him!'

'And was that it?' said my aunt. 'I heard something. . . .'

Eliza nodded.

'That affected his mind,' she said. 'After that he began to mope by himself, talking to no one and wandering about by himself. So one night he was wanted for to go on a call and they couldn't find him anywhere. They looked high up and low down; and still they couldn't see a sight of him anywhere. So then the clerk suggested to try the chapel. So then they got the keys and opened the chapel, and the clerk and Father O'Rourke and another priest that was there brought in a light for to look for him . . . And what do you think but there he was, sitting up by himself in the dark in his confession-box, wide-awake and laughing-like softly to himself?'

She stopped suddenly as if to listen. I too listened; but there was no sound in the house: and I knew that the old priest was lying still in his coffin as we had seen him, solemn and truculent in death, an idle chalice on his breast.

Eliza resumed:

'Wide awake and laughing-like to himself . . . So then, of course, when they saw that, that made them think that there was something gone wrong with him. . . .'

2
An Encounter

It was Joe Dillon who introduced the Wild West to us. He had a little library made up of old numbers of *The Union Jack, Pluck* and *The Halfpenny Marvel*.[1] Every evening after school we met in his back garden and arranged Indian battles. He and his fat young brother Leo, the idler, held the loft of the stable while we tried to carry it by storm; or we fought a pitched battle on the grass. But, however well we fought, we never won siege or battle and all our bouts ended with Joe Dillon's war dance of victory. His parents went to eight-o'clock mass every morning in Gardiner Street and the peaceful odour of Mrs Dillon was prevalent in the hall of the house. But he played too fiercely for us who were younger and more timid. He looked like some kind of an Indian when he capered round the garden, an old tea-cosy on his head, beating a tin with his fist and yelling:

'Ya! yaka, yaka, yaka!'

Everyone was incredulous when it was reported that he had a vocation for the priesthood. Nevertheless it was true.

A spirit of unruliness diffused itself among us and, under its influence, differences of culture and constitution were waived. We banded ourselves together, some boldly, some in jest and some almost in fear: and of the number of these latter, the reluctant Indians who were afraid to seem studious or lacking in robustness, I was one. The adventures related in the literature of the Wild West were remote from my nature but, at least, they opened doors of escape. I liked better some American detective stories which were traversed from time to time by unkempt fierce and beautiful girls. Though there was nothing wrong in these stories and though their intention was sometimes literary, they were circulated secretly at school. One day when Father Butler was hearing the four pages of Roman History, clumsy Leo Dillon was discovered with a copy of *The Halfpenny Marvel*.

'This page or this page? This page? Now, Dillon, up! "*Hardly had the day*" . . . Go on! What day? "*Hardly had the day dawned*"

[1] children's comics

. . . Have you studied it? What have you there in your pocket?'

Everyone's heart palpitated as Leo Dillon handed up the paper and everyone assumed an innocent face. Father Butler turned over the pages, frowning.

'What is this rubbish?' he said. '*The Apache Chief!* Is that what you read instead of studying your Roman History? Let me not find any more of this wretched stuff in this college. The man who wrote it, I suppose, was some wretched fellow who writes these things for a drink. I'm surprised at boys like you, educated, reading such stuff. I could understand it if you were . . . National School[1] boys. Now, Dillon, I advise you strongly, get at your work or . . .'

This rebuke during the sober hours of school paled much of the glory of the Wild West for me, and the confused puffy face of Leo Dillon awakened one of my consciences. But when the restraining influence of the school was at a distance I began to hunger again for wild sensations, for the escape which those chronicles of disorder alone seemed to offer me. The mimic warfare of the evening became at last as wearisome to me as the routine of school in the morning because I wanted real adventures to happen to myself. But real adventures, I reflected do not happen to people who remain at home: they must be sought abroad.

The summer holidays were near at hand when I made up my mind to break out of the weariness of school life for one day at least. With Leo Dillon and a boy named Mahony I planned a day's miching.[2] Each of us saved up sixpence. We were to meet at ten in the morning on the Canal Bridge. Mahony's big sister was to write an excuse for him and Leo Dillon was to tell his brother to say he was sick. We arranged to go along the Wharf Road until we came to the ships, then to cross in the ferryboat and walk out to see the Pigeon House. Leo Dillon was afraid we might meet Father Butler or someone out of the college; but Mahony asked, very sensibly, what would Father Butler be doing out at the Pigeon House. We were reassured, and I brought the first stage of the plot to an end by collecting sixpence from the other two, at the same time showing them my own sixpence. When we were making the last arrangements on

---

[1] National Schools were run by the state, and were thought to be poor schools. They were looked down on by those who could afford private education

[2] playing truant

the eve we were all vaguely excited. We shook hands, laughing, and Mahony said:

'Till tomorrow, mates!'

That night I slept badly. In the morning I was first-comer to the bridge, as I lived nearest. I hid my books in the long grass near the ashpit at the end of the garden where nobody ever came, and hurried along the canal bank. It was a mild sunny morning in the first week of June. I sat up on the coping of the bridge, admiring my frail canvas shoes which I had diligently pipeclayed[1] overnight and watching the docile horses pulling a tramload of business people up the hill. All the branches of the tall trees which lined the mall[2] were gay with little light green leaves, and the sunlight slanted through them onto the water. The granite stone of the bridge was beginning to be warm, and I began to pat it with my hands in time to an air in my head. I was very happy.

When I had been sitting there for five or ten minutes I saw Mahony's grey suit approaching. He came up the hill, smiling, and clambered up beside me on the bridge. While we were waiting he brought out the catapult which bulged from his inner pocket and explained some improvements which he had made in it. I asked him why he had brought it, and he told me he had brought it to have some gas[3] with the birds. Mahony used slang freely, and spoke of Father Butler as Old Bunser. We waited on for a quarter of an hour more, but still there was no sign of Leo Dillon. Mahony, at last, jumped down and said:

'Come along. I knew Fatty'd funk it.'

'And his sixpence . . . ?' I said.

'That's forfeit,' said Mahony. 'And so much the better for us – a bob and a tanner instead of a bob.'

We walked along the North Strand Road till we came to the Vitriol[4] Works and then turned to the right along the Wharf Road. Mahony began to play the Indian as soon as we were out of public sight. He chased a crowd of ragged girls, brandishing his unloaded catapult and, when two ragged boys began, out of chivalry, to fling stones at us, he proposed that we should charge them. I objected that the boys were too small, and so we walked

[1] whitened

[2] road

[3] fun (slang)

[4] sulphuric acid

on, the ragged troop screaming after us: '*Swaddlers! Swaddlers!*'[1]
thinking that we were Protestants because Mahony, who was
dark-complexioned, wore the silver badge of a cricket club in his
cap. When we came to the Smoothing Iron[2] we arranged a
siege; but it was a failure because you must have at least three.
We revenged ourselves on Leo Dillon by saying what a funk he
was and guessing how many he would get at three o'clock from
Mr Ryan.

We came then near the river. We spent a long time walking
about the noisy streets flanked by high stone walls, watching the
working of cranes and engines and often being shouted at for our
immobility by the drivers of groaning carts. It was noon when
we reached the quays and, as all the labourers seemed to be
eating their lunches, we bought two big currant buns and sat
down to eat them on some metal piping beside the river. We
pleased ourselves with the spectacle of Dublin's commerce – the
barges signalled from far away by their curls of woolly smoke,
the brown fishing fleet beyond Ringsend, the big white sailing
vessel which was being discharged on the opposite quay.
Mahony said it would be right skit to run away to sea on one of
those big ships, and even I, looking at the high masts, saw, or
imagined, the geography which had been scantily dosed to me at
school gradually taking substance under my eyes. School and
home seemed to recede from us and their influences upon us
seemed to wane.

We crossed the Liffey in the ferryboat, paying our toll to be
transported in the company of two labourers and a little Jew
with a bag. We were serious to the point of solemnity, but once
during the short voyage our eyes met and we laughed. When we
landed we watched the discharging of the graceful three-master
which we had observed from the other quay. Some bystander
said that she was a Norwegian vessel. I went to the stern and
tried to decipher the legend upon it but, failing to do so, I came
back and examined the foreign sailors to see had any of them
green eyes for I had some confused notion . . . The sailors' eyes
were blue, and grey, and even black. The only sailor whose eyes
could have been called green was a tall man who amused the
crowd on the quay by calling out cheerfully every time the
planks fell:

[1] Protestants (slang)

[2] a building in Dublin resembling a flat iron in its shape

'All right! All right!'

When we were tired of this sight we wandered slowly into Ringsend. The day had grown sultry, and in the windows of the grocers' shops musty biscuits lay bleaching. We bought some biscuits and chocolate, which we ate sedulously as we wandered through the squalid streets where the families of the fishermen live. We could find no dairy and so we went into a huckster's[1] shop and bought a bottle of raspberry lemonade each. Refreshed by this, Mahony chased a cat down a lane, but the cat escaped into a wide field. We both felt rather tired, and when we reached the field we made at once for a sloping bank, over the ridge of which we could see the Dodder.[2]

It was too late and we were too tired to carry out our project of visiting the Pigeon House. We had to be home before four o'clock, lest our adventures should be discovered. Mahony looked regretfully at his catapult, and I had to suggest going home by train before he regained any cheerfulness. The sun went in behind some clouds and left us to our jaded thoughts and the crumbs of our provisions.

There was nobody but ourselves in the field. When we had lain on the bank for some time without speaking I saw a man approaching from the far end of the field. I watched him lazily as I chewed one of those green stems on which girls tell fortunes. He came along by the bank slowly. He walked with one hand upon his hip and in the other hand he held a stick with which he tapped the turf lightly. He was shabbily dressed in a suit of greenish-black and wore what we used to call a jerry hat with a high crown. He seemed to be fairly old, for his moustache was ashen-grey. When he passed at our feet he glanced up at us quickly and then continued his way. We followed him with our eyes and saw that when he had gone on for perhaps fifty paces he turned about and began to retrace his steps. He walked towards us very slowly, always tapping the ground with his stick, so slowly that I thought he was looking for something in the grass.

He stopped when he came level with us and bade us good-day. We answered him, and he sat down beside us on the slope slowly and with great care. He began to talk of the weather, saying that it would be a very hot summer and adding that the

[1] shopkeeper selling only small items

[2] one of the rivers running through Dublin

seasons had changed greatly since he was a boy – a long time ago. He said that the happiest time of one's life was undoubtedly one's schoolboy days, and that he would give anything to be young again. While he expressed these sentiments, which bored us a little, we kept silent. Then he began to talk of school and of books. He asked us whether we had read the poetry of Thomas Moore or the works of Sir Walter Scott and Lord Lytton. I pretended that I had read every book he mentioned, so that in the end he said:

'Ah, I can see you are a bookworm like myself. Now,' he added, pointing to Mahony who was regarding us with open eyes, 'he is different; he goes in for games.'

He said he had all Sir Walter Scott's works and all Lord Lytton's works at home and never tired of reading them. 'Of course,' he said, 'there were some of Lord Lytton's works which boys couldn't read.' Mahony asked why couldn't boys read them – a question which agitated and pained me because I was afraid the man would think I was as stupid as Mahony. The man, however, only smiled. I saw that he had great gaps in his mouth between his yellow teeth. Then he asked us which of us had the most sweethearts. Mahony mentioned lightly that he had three totties. The man asked me how many I had. I answered that I had none. He did not believe me and said he was sure I must have one. I was silent.

'Tell us,' said Mahony pertly to the man, 'how many have you yourself?'

The man smiled as before and said that when he was our age he had lots of sweethearts.

'Every boy,' he said, 'has a little sweetheart.'

His attitude at this point struck me as strangely liberal in a man of his age. In my heart I thought that what he said about boys and sweethearts was reasonable. But I disliked the words in his mouth, and I wondered why he shivered once or twice as if he feared something or felt a sudden chill. As he proceeded I noticed that his accent was good. He began to speak to us about girls, saying what nice soft hair they had and how soft their hands were and how all girls were not so good as they seemed to be if one only knew. There was nothing he liked, he said, so much as looking at a nice young girl, at her nice white hands and her beautiful soft hair. He gave me the impression that he was repeating something which he had learned by heart or that, magnetized by some words of his own speech, his mind was slowly circling round and round in the same orbit. At times he spoke as if he were simply alluding to some fact that everybody knew, and at times he lowered his voice and spoke mysteriously as if he were telling us something secret which he did not wish others to overhear. He repeated his phrases over and over again, varying them and surrounding them with his monotonous voice. I continued to gaze towards the foot of the slope, listening to him.

After a long while his monologue paused. He stood up slowly, saying that he had to leave us for a minute or so, a few minutes, and, without changing the direction of my gaze, I saw him walking slowly away from us towards the near end of the field. We remained silent when he had gone. After a silence of a few minutes I heard Mahony exclaim:

'I say! Look what he's doing!'

As I neither answered nor raised my eyes, Mahony exclaimed again:

'I say . . . He's a queer old josser!'[1]

'In case he asks us for our names,' I said, 'let you be Murphy and I'll be Smith.'

We said nothing further to each other. I was still considering whether I would go away or not when the man came back and sat down beside us again. Hardly had he sat down when Mahony, catching sight of the cat which had escaped him, sprang up and pursued her across the field. The man and I watched the chase. The cat escaped once more and Mahony began to throw stones at the wall she had escaladed. Desisting from this, he began to wander about the far end of the field, aimlessly.

After an interval the man spoke to me. He said that my friend was a very rough boy, and asked did he get whipped often at school. I was going to reply indignantly that we were not National School boys to be whipped, as he called it; but I remained silent. He began to speak on the subject of chastising boys. His mind, as if magnetized again by his speech, seemed to circle slowly round and round its new centre. He said that when boys were that kind they ought to be whipped and well whipped. When a boy was rough and unruly there was nothing would do him any good but a good sound whipping. A slap on the hand or a box on the ear was no good: what he wanted was to get a nice warm whipping. I was surprised at this sentiment and involun-

[1] fellow

tarily glanced up at his face. As I did so I met the gaze of a pair of bottle-green eyes peering at me from under a twitching forehead. I turned my eyes away again.

The man continued his monologue. He seemed to have forgotten his recent liberalism. He said that if ever he found a boy talking to girls or having a girl for a sweetheart he would whip him and whip him; and that would teach him not to be talking to girls. And if a boy had a girl for a sweetheart and told lies about it, then he would give him such a whipping as no boy ever got in this world. He said that there was nothing in this world he would like so well as that. He described to me how he would whip such a boy, as if he were unfolding some elaborate mystery. He would love that, he said, better than anything in this world; and his voice, as he led me monotonously through the mystery, grew almost affectionate and seemed to plead with me that I should understand him.

I waited till his monologue paused again. Then I stood up abruptly. Lest I should betray my agitation I delayed a few moments, pretending to fix my shoe properly, and then, saying that I was obliged to go, I bade him good day. I went up the slope calmly but my heart was beating quickly with fear that he would seize me by the ankles. When I reached the top of the slope I turned round and, without looking at him, called loudly across the field:

'Murphy!'

My voice had an accent of forced bravery in it, and I was ashamed of my paltry stratagem. I had to call the name again before Mahony saw me and hallooed in answer. Now my heart beat as he came running across the field to me! He ran as if to bring me aid. And I was penitent; for in my heart I had always despised him a little.

3
The Pandying

Father Arnall came in and the Latin lesson began and he remained still leaning on the desk with his arms folded. Father Arnall gave out the themebooks[1] and he said that they were scandalous and that they were all to be written out again with the corrections at once. But the worst of all was Fleming's theme because the pages were stuck together by a blot: and Father Arnall held it up by a corner and said it was an insult to any master to send him up such a theme.[2] Then he asked Jack Lawton to decline the noun *mare* and Jack Lawton stopped at the ablative singular and could not go on with the plural.

– You should be ashamed of yourself, said Father Arnall sternly. You, the leader of the class!

Then he asked the next boy and the next and the next. Nobody knew. Father Arnall became very quiet, more and more quiet as each boy tried to answer it and could not. But his face was black looking and his eyes were staring though his voice was so quiet. Then he asked Fleming and Fleming said that that word had no plural. Father Arnall suddenly shut the book and shouted at him:

– Kneel out there in the middle of the class. You are one of the idlest boys I ever met. Copy out your themes again the rest of you.

Fleming moved heavily out of his place and knelt between the two last benches. The other boys bent over their themebooks and began to write. A silence filled the classroom and Stephen, glancing timidly at Father Arnall's dark face, saw that it was a little red from the wax he was in.

Was that a sin for Father Arnall to be in a wax or was he allowed to get into a wax when the boys were idle because that made them study better or was he only letting on[3] to be in a wax? It was because he was allowed, because a priest would

[1] exercise books

[2] essay or exercise

[3] pretending

know what a sin was and would not do it. But if he did it one time by mistake what would he do to go to confession? Perhaps he would go to confession to the minister. And if the minister did it he would go to the rector: and the rector to the provincial: and the provincial to the general of the jesuits. That was called the order: and he had heard his father say that they were all clever men. They could all have become high-up people in the world if they had not become jesuits. And he wondered what Father Arnall and Paddy Barrett would have become and what Mr McGlade and Mr Gleeson would have become if they had not become jesuits. It was hard to think what because you would have to think of them in a different way with different coloured coats and trousers and with beards and moustaches and different kinds of hats.

The door opened quietly and closed. A quick whisper ran through the class: the prefect of studies.[1] There was an instant of dead silence and then the loud crack of a pandybat[2] on the last desk. Stephen's heart leapt up in fear.

– Any boys want flogging here, Father Arnall? cried the prefect of studies. Any lazy idle loafers that want flogging in this class?

He came to the middle of the class and saw Fleming on his knees.

– Hoho! he cried. Who is this boy? Why is he on his knees? What is your name, boy?

– Fleming, sir.

– Hoho, Fleming! An idler of course. I can see it in your eye. Why is he on his knees, Father Arnall?

– He wrote a bad Latin theme, Father Arnall said, and he missed all the questions in grammar.

– Of course he did! cried the prefect of studies, of course he did! A born idler! I can see it in the corner of his eye.

He banged his pandybat down on the desk and cried:

– Up, Fleming! Up, my boy!

Fleming stood up slowly.

– Hold out! cried the prefect of studies.

Fleming held out his hand. The pandybat came down on it with a loud smacking sound: one, two, three, four, five, six.

– Other hand!

[1] teacher in charge of school studies and discipline

[2] stick used for punishment in school

The pandybat came down again in six loud quick smacks.

– Kneel down! cried the prefect of studies.

Fleming knelt down squeezing his hands under his armpits, his face contorted with pain, but Stephen knew how hard his hands were because Fleming was always rubbing rosin into them. But perhaps he was in great pain for the noise of the pandybat was terrible. Stephen's heart was beating and fluttering.

– At your work, all of you! shouted the prefect of studies. We want no lazy idle loafers here, lazy idle little schemers. At your work, I tell you. Father Dolan will be in to see you every day. Father Dolan will be in tomorrow.

He poked one of the boys in the side with the pandybat, saying:

– You, boy! When will Father Dolan be in again?

– Tomorrow, sir, said Tom Furlong's voice.

– Tomorrow and tomorrow and tomorrow, said the prefect of studies. Make up your minds for that. Every day Father Dolan. Write away. You boy, who are you?

Stephen's heart jumped suddenly.

– Dedalus, sir.

– Why are you not writing like the others?

– I . . . my . . .

He could not speak with fright.

– Why is he not writing, Father Arnall?

– He broke his glasses, said Father Arnall, and I exempted him from work.

– Broke? What is this I hear? What is this? Your name is? said the prefect of studies.

– Dedalus, sir.

– Out here, Dedalus. Lazy little schemer. I see schemer in your face. Where did you break your glasses?

Stephen stumbled into the middle of the class, blinded by fear and haste.

– Where did you break your glasses? repeated the prefect of studies.

– The cinderpath, sir.

– Hoho! The cinderpath! cried the prefect of studies. I know that trick.

Stephen lifted his eyes in wonder and saw for a moment Father Dolan's whitegrey not young face, his baldy whitegrey head with fluff at the sides of it, the steel rims of his spectacles and his nocoloured eyes looking through the glasses. Why did he say he knew that trick?

– Lazy idle little loafer! cried the prefect of studies. Broke my glasses! An old schoolboy trick! Out with your hand this moment!

Stephen closed his eyes and held out in the air his trembling hand with the palm upwards. He felt the prefect of studies touch it for a moment at the fingers to straighten it and then the swish of the sleeve of the soutane[1] as the pandybat was lifted to strike. A hot burning stinging tingling blow like the loud crack of a broken stick made his trembling hand crumple together like a leaf in the fire: and at the sound and the pain scalding tears were driven into his eyes. His whole body was shaking with fright, his arm was shaking and his crumpled burning livid hand shook like a loose leaf in the air. A cry sprang to his lips, a prayer to be let off. But though the tears scalded his eyes and his limbs quivered with pain and fright he held back the hot tears and the cry that scalded the throat.

– Other hand! shouted the prefect of studies.

Stephen drew back his maimed and quivering right arm and held out his left hand. The soutane sleeve swished again as the pandybat was lifted and a loud crashing sound and a fierce maddening tingling burning pain made his hand shrink together with the palms and fingers in a livid quivering mass. The scalding water burst forth from his eyes and, burning with shame and agony and fear, he drew back his shaking arm in terror and burst out in a whine of pain. His body shook with a palsy of fright and in shame and rage he felt the scalding cry come from his throat and the scalding tears falling out of his eyes and down his flaming cheeks.

– Kneel down! cried the prefect of studies.

Stephen knelt down quickly pressing his beaten hands to his sides. To think of them beaten and swollen with pain all in a moment made him feel so sorry for them as if they were not his own but someone else's that he felt sorry for. And as he knelt, calming the last sobs in his throat and feeling the burning tingling pain pressed into his sides, he thought of the hands which he had held out in the air with the palms up and of the firm touch of the prefect of studies when he had steadied the shaking fingers and of the beaten swollen reddened mass of palm

[1] cassock, long black robe worn by a priest

and fingers that shook helplessly in the air.

– Get at your work, all of you, cried the prefect of studies from the door. Father Dolan will be in every day to see if any boy, any lazy idle little loafer wants flogging. Every day. Every day.

The door closed behind him.

The hushed class continued to copy out the themes. Father Arnall rose from his seat and went among them, helping the boys with gentle words and telling them the mistakes they had made. His voice was very gentle and soft. Then he returned to his seat and said to Fleming and Stephen:

– You may return to your places, you two.

Fleming and Stephen rose and walking to their seats, sat down. Stephen, scarlet with shame, opened a book quickly with one weak hand and bent down upon it, his face close to the page.

It was unfair and cruel because the doctor had told him not to read without glasses and he had written home to his father that morning to send him a new pair. And Father Arnall had said that he need not study till the new glasses came. Then to be called a schemer before the class and to be pandied when he always got the card for first or second and was the leader of the Yorkists! How could the prefect of studies know that it was a trick? He felt the touch of the prefect's fingers as they had steadied his hand and at first he had thought he was going to shake hands with him because the fingers were soft and firm: but then in an instant he had heard the swish of the soutane sleeve and the crash. It was cruel and unfair to make him kneel in the middle of the class then: and Father Arnall had told them both that they might return to their places without making any difference between them. He listened to Father Arnall's low and gentle voice as he corrected the themes. Perhaps he was sorry now and wanted to be decent. But it was unfair and cruel. The prefect of studies was a priest but that was cruel and unfair. And his whitegrey face and the nocoloured eyes behind the steel-rimmed spectacles were cruel looking because he had steadied the hand first with his firm soft fingers and that was to hit it better and louder.

– It's a stinking mean thing, that's what it is, said Fleming in the corridor as the classes were passing out in file to the refectory,[1] to pandy a fellow for what is not his fault.

– You really broke your glasses by accident, didn't you?

[1] dining hall

Nasty Roche asked.

Stephen felt his heart filled by Fleming's words and did not answer.

– Of course he did! said Fleming. I wouldn't stand it. I'd go up and tell the rector on him.

– Yes, said Cecil Thunder eagerly, and I saw him lift the pandybat over his shoulder and he's not allowed to do that.

– Did it hurt much? Nasty Roche asked.

– Very much, Stephen said.

– I wouldn't stand it, Fleming repeated, from Baldyhead or any other Baldyhead. It's a stinking mean low trick, that's what it is. I'd go straight up to the rector and tell him about it after dinner.

– Yes, do. Yes, do, said Cecil Thunder.

– Yes, do. Yes, go up and tell the rector on him, Dedalus, said Nasty Roche, because he said that he'd come in tomorrow again and pandy you.

– Yes, yes. Tell the rector, all said.

And there were some fellows out of second of grammar[1] listening and one of them said:

– The senate and the Roman people declared that Dedalus had been wrongly punished.

It was wrong; it was unfair and cruel: and, as he sat in the refectory, he suffered time after time in memory the same humiliation until he began to wonder whether it might not really be that there was something in his face which made him look like a schemer and he wished he had a little mirror to see. But there could not be; and it was unjust and cruel and unfair.

He could not eat the blackish fish fritters they got on Wednesdays in Lent and one of his potatoes had the mark of the spade in it. Yes, he would do what the fellows had told him. He would go up and tell the rector that he had been wrongly punished. A thing like that had been done before by somebody in history, by some great person whose head was in the books of history. And the rector would declare that he had been wrongly punished because the senate and the Roman people always declared that the men who did that had been wrongly punished. Those were the great men whose names were in Richmal Magnall's Questions.[2] History was all about those men and what they did and that was what Peter Parley's Tales about Greece and Rome[2]

[1] one of the forms in which Latin and Roman history are the principal subjects
[2] schoolbooks used in the late nineteenth century

were all about. Peter Parley himself was on the first page in a picture. There was a road over a heath with grass at the side and little bushes: and Peter Parley had a broad hat like a protestant minister and a big stick and he was walking fast along the road to Greece and Rome.

It was easy what he had to do. All he had to do was when the dinner was over and he came out in his turn to go on walking but not out to the corridor but up the staircase on the right that led to the castle.[1] He had nothing to do but that; to turn to the right and walk fast up the staircase and in half a minute he would be in the low dark narrow corridor that led through the castle to the rector's room. And every fellow had said that it was unfair, even the fellow out of second of grammar who had said that about the senate and the Roman people.

What would happen? He heard the fellows of the higher line stand up at the top of the refectory and heard their steps as they came down the matting: Paddy Rath and Jimmy Magee and the Spaniard and the Portuguese and the fifth was big Corrigan who was going to be flogged by Mr Gleeson. That was why the prefect of studies had called him a schemer and pandied him for nothing: and, straining his weak eyes, tired with the tears, he watched big Corrigan's broad shoulders and big hanging black head passing in the file. But he had done something and besides Mr Gleeson would not flog him hard: and he remembered how big Corrigan looked in the bath. He had skin the same colour as the turf-coloured bogwater in the shallow end of the bath and when he walked along the side his feet slapped loudly on the wet-tiles and at every step his thighs shook a little because he was fat.

The refectory was half empty and the fellows were still passing out in file. He could go up the staircase because there was never a priest or a prefect outside the refectory door. But he could not go. The rector would side with the prefect of studies and think it was a schoolboy trick and then the prefect of studies would come in every day the same, only it would be worse because he would be dreadfully waxy at any fellow going up to the rector about him. The fellows had told him to go but they would not go themselves. They had forgotten all about it. No, it was best to forget all about it and perhaps the prefect of studies had only said he would come in. No, it was best to hide out of the way

[1] the school-buildings at Clongowes were built on to an old castle

because when you were small and young you could often escape that way.

The fellows at his table stood up. He stood up and passed out among them in the file. He had to decide. He was coming near the door. If he went on with the fellows he could never go up to the rector because he could not leave the playground for that. And if he went and was pandied all the same all the fellows would make fun and talk about young Dedalus going up to the rector to tell on the prefect of studies.

He was walking down along the matting and he saw the door before him. It was impossible: he could not. He thought of the baldy head of the prefect of studies with the cruel nocoloured eyes looking at him and he heard the voice of the prefect of studies asking him twice what his name was. Why could he not remember the name when he was told the first time? Was he not listening the first time or was it to make fun out of the name? The great men in the history had names like that and nobody made fun of them. It was his own name that he should have made fun of if he wanted to make fun. Dolan: it was like the name of a woman who washed clothes.

He had reached the door and, turning quickly up to the right, walked up the stairs; and, before he could make up his mind to come back, he had entered the low dark narrow corridor that led to the castle. And as he crossed the threshold of the door of the corridor he saw, without turning his head to look, that all the fellows were looking after him as they went filing by.

He passed along the narrow dark corridor, passing little doors that were the doors of the rooms of the community.[1] He peered in front of him and right and left through the gloom and thought that those must be portraits. It was dark and silent and his eyes were weak and tired with tears so that he could not see. But he thought they were the portraits of the saints and great men of the order[2] who were looking down on him silently as he passed: saint Ignatius Loyola holding an open book and pointing to the words *Ad Majorem Dei Gloriam*[3] in it, saint Francis Xavier pointing to his chest, Lorenzo Ricci with his biretta[4] on his head

---

[1] the Jesuit priests who taught at the school

[2] saints and notable men associated with the Society of Jesus throughout its history

[3] 'To the Greater Glory of God'

[4] a square hat or cap worn by members of the clergy

like one of the prefects of the lines, the three patrons of holy
youth, saint Stanislaus Kostka, saint Aloysius Gonzaga and
Blessed John Berchmans, all with young faces because they died
when they were young, and Father Peter Kenny sitting in a
chair wrapped in a big cloak.

He came out on the landing above the entrance hall and
looked about him. That was where Hamilton Rowan had passed
and the marks of the soldiers' slugs were there. And it was there
that the old servants had seen the ghost in the white cloak of a
marshal.

An old servant was sweeping at the end of the landing. He
asked him where was the rector's room and the old servant
pointed to the door at the far end and looked after him as he
went on to it and knocked.

There was no answer. He knocked again more loudly and his
heart jumped when he heard a muffled voice say:

– Come in!

He turned the handle and opened the door and fumbled for
the handle of the green baize door inside. He found it and
pushed it open and went in.

He saw the rector sitting at a desk writing. There was a skull
on the desk and a strange solemn smell in the room like the old
leather of chairs.

His heart was beating fast on account of the solemn place he
was in and the silence of the room: and he looked at the skull
and at the rector's kindlooking face.

– Well, my little man, said the rector, what is it?

Stephen swallowed down the thing in this throat and said:

– I broke my glasses, sir.

The rector opened his mouth and said:

– O!

Then he smiled and said:

– Well, if we broke our glasses we must write home for a new pair.

– I wrote home, sir, said Stephen, and Father Arnall said I am
not to study till they come.

– Quite right! said the rector.

Stephen swallowed down the thing again and tried to keep his
legs and his voice from shaking.

– But, sir. . . .

– Yes?

— Father Dolan came in today and pandied me because I was
not writing my theme.

The rector looked at him in silence and he could feel the blood rising to his face and the tears about to rise to his eyes.

The rector said:

– Your name is Dedalus, isn't it?

– Yes, sir.

– And where did you break your glasses?

– On the cinderpath, sir. A fellow was coming out of the bicycle house and I fell and they got broken. I don't know the fellow's name.

The rector looked at him again in silence. Then he smiled and said:

– O, well, it was a mistake; I am sure Father Dolan did not know.

– But I told him I broke them, sir, and he pandied me.

– Did you tell him that you had written home for a new pair? the rector asked.

– No, sir.

– O well then, said the rector, Father Dolan did not understand. You can say that I excuse you from your lessons for a few days.

Stephen said quickly for fear his trembling would prevent him:

– Yes, sir, but Father Dolan said he will come in tomorrow to pandy me again for it.

– Very well, the rector said, it is a mistake and I shall speak to Father Dolan myself. Will that do now?

Stephen felt the tears wetting his eyes and murmured:

– O yes sir, thanks.

The rector held his hand across the side of the desk where the skull was and Stephen, placing his hand in it for a moment, felt a cool moist palm.

– Good day now, said the rector, withdrawing his hand and bowing.

– Good day, sir, said Stephen.

He bowed and walked quietly out of the room, closing the doors carefully and slowly.

But when he had passed the old servant on the landing and was again in the low narrow dark corridor he began to walk faster and faster. Faster and faster he hurried on through the gloom excitedly. He bumped his elbow against the door at the end and, hurrying down the staircase, walked quickly through the two corridors and out into the air.

He could hear the cries of the fellows on the playgrounds. He broke into a run and, running quicker and quicker, ran across the cinderpath and reached the third line playground, panting.

The fellows had seen him running. They closed round him in a ring, pushing one against another to hear.

– Tell us! Tell us!

– What did he say?

– Did you go in?

– What did he say?

– Tell us! Tell us!

He told them what he had said and what the rector had said, and when he had told them, all the fellows flung their caps spinning up into the air and cried:

– Hurroo!

They caught their caps and sent them up again spinning sky-high and cried again:

– Hurroo! Hurroo!

They made a cradle of their locked hands and hoisted him up among them and carried him along till he struggled to get free. And when he had escaped from them they broke away in all directions, flinging their caps again into the air and whistling as they went spinning and crying:

– Hurroo!

And they gave three groans for Baldyhead Dolan and three cheers for Conmee and they said he was the decentest rector that was ever in Clongowes.

The cheers died away in the soft grey air. He was alone. He was happy and free: but he would not be anyway proud with Father Dolan. He would be very quiet and obedient: and he wished that he could do something kind for him to show him that he was not proud.

The air was soft and grey and mild and evening was coming. There was the smell of evening in the air, the smell of the fields in the country where they digged up turnips to peel them and eat them when they went out for a walk to Major Barton's, the smell there was in the little wood beyond the pavilion where the gall-nuts[1] were.

The fellows were practising long shies and bowling lobs and slow twisters. In the soft grey silence he could hear the bump of

[1] nut-shaped growths produced on oak trees by the gall-wasp and at one time used in ink-making

the balls: and from here and from there through the quiet air the sound of the cricket bats: pick, pack, pock, puck: like drops of water in a fountain falling softly in the brimming bowl.

Loves and Conflicts

4
Araby

North Richmond Street, being blind, was a quiet street except at the hour when the Christian Brothers' School set the boys free. An uninhabited house of two storeys stood at the blind end, detached from its neighbours in a square ground. The other houses of the street, conscious of decent lives within them, gazed at one another with brown imperturbable faces.

The former tenant of our house, a priest, had died in the back drawing-room. Air, musty from having been long enclosed, hung in all the rooms, and the waste room behind the kitchen was littered with old useless papers. Among these I found a few paper-covered books, the pages of which were curled and damp: *The Abbot*, by Walter Scott, *The Devout Communicant* and *The Memoirs of Vidocq*. I liked the last best because its leaves were yellow. The wild garden behind the house contained a central apple tree and a few straggling bushes, under one of which I found the late tenant's rusty bicycle-pump. He had been a very charitable priest; in his will he had left all his money to institutions and the furniture of his house to his sister.

When the short days of winter came, dusk fell before we had well eaten our dinners. When we met in the street the houses had grown sombre. The space of sky above us was the colour of ever-changing violet and towards it the lamps of the street lifted their feeble lanterns. The cold air stung us and we played till our bodies glowed. Our shouts echoed in the silent street. The career of our play brought us through the dark muddy lanes behind the houses, where we ran the gauntlet of the rough tribes from the cottages, to the back doors of the dark dripping gardens where odours arose from the ashpits, to the dark odorous stables where a coachman smoothed and combed the horse or shook music from the buckled harness. When we returned to the street, light from the kitchen windows had filled the areas. If my uncle was seen turning the corner, we hid in the shadow until we had seen him safely housed. Or if Mangan's sister came out on the door-step to call her brother in to his tea, we watched her from our shadow peer up and down the street. We waited to see whether she would remain or go in and, if she remained, we left our shadow and walked up to Mangan's steps resignedly. She was waiting for us, her figure defined by the light from the half-opened door. Her brother always teased her before he obeyed, and I stood by the railings looking at her. Her dress swung as she moved her body, and the soft rope of her hair tossed from side to side.

Every morning I lay on the floor in the front parlour watching her door. The blind was pulled down to within an inch of the sash so that I could not be seen. When she came out on the doorstep my heart leaped. I ran to the hall, seized my books and followed her. I kept her brown figure always in my eye and, when we came near the point at which our ways diverged, I quickened my pace and passed her. This happened morning after morning. I had never spoken to her, except for a few casual words, and yet her name was like a summons to all my foolish blood.

Her image accompanied me even in places the most hostile to romance. On Saturday evenings when my aunt went marketing I had to go to carry some of the parcels. We walked through the flaring streets, jostled by drunken men and bargaining women, amid the curses of labourers, the shrill litanies of shop-boys who stood on guard by the barrels of pigs' cheeks, the nasal chanting of street-singers, who sang a *come-all-you*[1] about O'Donovan Rossa,[2] or a ballad about the troubles in our native land. These noises converged in a single sensation of life for me: I imagined that I bore my chalice safely through a throng of foes. Her name sprang to my lips at moments in strange prayers and praises which I myself did not understand. My eyes were often full of tears (I could not tell why) and at times a flood from my heart seemed to pour itself out into my bosom. I thought little of the future. I did not know whether I would ever speak to her or not or, if I spoke to her, how I would tell her of my confused adoration. But my body was like a harp and her words and gestures were like fingers running upon the wires.

One evening I went into the back drawing-room in which the priest had died. It was a dark rainy evening and there was no sound in the house. Through one of the broken panes I heard the rain impinge upon the earth, the fine incessant needles of water

---

[1] a song (especially a folk ballad) in which the words 'come all you' recur
[2] an Irish patriot

playing in the sodden beds. Some distant lamp or lighted window gleamed below me. I was thankful that I could see so little. All my senses seemed to desire to veil themselves and, feeling that I was about to slip from them, I pressed the palms of my hands together until they trembled, murmuring: '*O love! O love!*' many times.

At last she spoke to me. When she addressed the first words to me I was so confused that I did not know what to answer. She asked me was I going to *Araby*. I forgot whether I answered yes or no. It would be a splendid bazaar, she said she would love to go.

'And why can't you?' I asked.

While she spoke she turned a silver bracelet round and round her wrist. She could not go, she said, because there would be a retreat[1] that week in her convent. Her brother and two other boys were fighting for their caps and I was alone at the railings. She held one of the spikes, bowing her head towards me. The light from the lamp opposite our door caught the white curve of her neck, lit up her hair that rested there and, falling, lit up the hand upon the railing. It fell over one side of her dress and caught the white border of a petticoat, just visible as she stood at ease.

'It's well for you,' she said.

'If I go,' I said. 'I will bring you something.'

What innumerable follies laid waste my waking and sleeping thoughts after that evening! I wished to annihilate the tedious intervening days. I chafed against the work of school. At night in my bedroom and by day in the classroom her image came between me and the page I strove to read. The syllables of the word *Araby* were called to me through the silence in which my soul luxuriated and cast an Eastern enchantment over me. I asked for leave to go to the bazaar on Saturday night. My aunt was surprised and hoped it was not some Freemason affair. I answered few questions in class. I watched my master's face pass from amiability to sternness; he hoped I was not beginning to idle. I could not call my wandering thoughts together. I had hardly any patience with the serious work of life which, now that it stood between me and my desire, seemed to me child's play, ugly monotonous child's play.

On Saturday morning I reminded my uncle that I wished to

[1] retirement for a period of religious meditation

go to the bazaar in the evening. He was fussing at the hallstand, looking for the hat-brush, and answered me curtly:

'Yes, boy, I know.'

As he was in the hall I could not go into the front parlour and lie at the window. I left the house in bad humour and walked slowly towards the school. The air was pitilessly raw and already my heart misgave me.

When I came home to dinner my uncle had not yet been home. Still it was early. I sat staring at the clock for some time and, when its ticking began to irritate me, I left the room. I mounted the staircase and gained the upper part of the house. The high, cold, empty, gloomy rooms liberated me and I went from room to room singing. From the front window I saw my companions playing below in the street. Their cries reached me weakened and indistinct and, leaning my forehead against the cool glass, I looked over at the dark house where she lived. I may have stood there for an hour, seeing nothing but a brown-clad figure cast by my imagination, touched discreetly by the lamp-light at the curved neck, at the hand upon the railings and at the border below the dress.

When I came downstairs again I found Mrs Mercer sitting at the fire. She was an old, garrulous woman, a pawnbroker's widow, who collected used stamps for some pious purpose. I had to endure the gossip of the tea-table. The meal was prolonged beyond an hour and still my uncle did not come in. Mrs Mercer stood up to go: she was sorry she couldn't wait any longer, but it was after eight o'clock and she did not like to be out late, as the night air was bad for her. When she had gone I began to walk up and down the room, clenching my fists. My aunt said:

'I'm afraid you may put off your bazaar for this night of Our Lord.'

At nine o'clock I heard my uncle's latchkey in the hall door. I heard him talking to himself and heard the hallstand rocking when it had received the weight of his overcoat. I could interpret these signs. When he was midway through his dinner I asked him to give me the money to go to the bazaar. He had forgotten.

'The people are in bed and after their first sleep now,' he said.

I did not smile. My aunt said to him energetically:

'Can't you give him the money and let him go? You've kept him late enough as it is.'

My uncle said he was very sorry he had forgotten. He said he believed in the old saying: 'All work and no play makes Jack a dull boy.' He asked me where I was going and, when I had told him a second time, he asked me did I know *The Arab's Farewell to his Steed*.[1] When I left the kitchen he was about to recite the opening lines of the piece to my aunt.

I held a florin[2] tightly in my hand as I strode down Bucking-ham Street towards the station. The sight of the streets thronged with buyers and glaring with gas recalled to me the purpose of my journey. I took my seat in a third-class carriage of a deserted train. After an intolerable delay the train moved out of the station slowly. It crept onward among ruinous houses and over the twinkling river. At Westland Row Station a crowd of people pressed to the carriage doors; but the porters moved them back, saying that it was a special train for the bazaar. I remained alone in the bare carriage. In a few minutes the train drew up beside an improvised wooden platform. I passed out on to the road and saw by the lighted dial of a clock that it was ten minutes to ten. In front of me was a large building which displayed the magical name.

I could not find any sixpenny entrance and, fearing that the bazaar would be closed, I passed in quickly through a turnstile, handing a shilling[3] to a weary-looking man. I found myself in a big hall girdled at half its height by a gallery. Nearly all the stalls were closed and the greater part of the hall was in darkness. I recognized a silence like that which pervades a church after a service. I walked into the centre of the bazaar timidly. A few people were gathered about the stalls which were still open. Before a curtain, over which the words *Café Chantant*[4] were written in coloured lamps, two men were counting money on a salver. I listened to the fall of the coins.

Remembering with difficulty why I had come I went over to one of the stalls and examined porcelain vases and flowered tea-sets. At the door of the stall a young lady was talking and laughing with two young gentlemen. I remarked their English accents and listened vaguely to their conversation.

'O, I never said such a thing?'

'O, but you did!'

[1] popular Victorian poem by Mrs Caroline Norton

[2] **two shillings** (ten new pence)

[3] twelve old pence (five new pence)

[4] a café or restaurant where singing is provided as an entertainment

'O, but I didn't!'

'Didn't she say that?'

'Yes. I heard her.'

'O, there's a . . . fib!'

Observing me, the young lady came over and asked me did I wish to buy anything. The tone of her voice was not encouraging; she seemed to have spoken to me out of a sense of duty. I looked humbly at the great jars that stood like eastern guards at either side of the dark entrance to the stall and murmured:

'No, thank you.'

The young lady changed the position of one of the vases and went back to the two young men. They began to talk of the same subject. Once or twice the young lady glanced at me over her shoulder.

I lingered before her stall, though I knew my stay was useless, to make my interest in her wares seem the more real. Then I turned away slowly and walked down the middle of the bazaar. I allowed the two pennies to fall against the sixpence in my pocket. I heard a voice call from one end of the gallery that the light was out. The upper part of the hall was now completely dark.

Gazing up into the darkness I saw myself as a creature driven and derided by vanity; and my eyes burned with anguish and anger.

5
Visits

Two great yellow caravans had halted one morning before the door and men had come tramping into the house to dismantle it. The furniture had been hustled out through the front garden which was strewn with wisps of straw and rope ends and into the huge vans at the gate. When all had been safely stowed the vans had set off noisily down the avenue: and from the window of the railway carriage, in which he had sat with his red-eyed mother, Stephen had seen them lumbering along the Merrion Road.

The parlour fire would not draw that evening and Mr Dedalus rested the poker against the bars of the grate to attract the flame. Uncle Charles dozed in a corner of the half furnished uncarpeted room and near him the family portraits leaned against the wall. The lamp on the table shed a weak light over the boarded floor, muddied by the feet of the vanmen. Stephen sat on a footstool beside his father listening to a long and incoherent monologue. He understood little or nothing of it at first but he became slowly aware that his father had enemies and that some fight was going to take place. He felt, too, that he was being enlisted for the fight, that some duty was being laid upon his shoulders. The sudden flight from the comfort and reverie of Blackrock, the passage through the gloomy foggy city, the thought of the bare cheerless house in which they were now to live made his heart heavy: and again an intuition, a foreknowledge of the future came to him. He understood also why the servants had often whispered together in the hall and why his father had often stood on the hearthrug, with his back to the fire, talking loudly to uncle Charles who urged him to sit down and eat his dinner.

– There's a crack of the whip left in me yet, Stephen, old chap, said Mr Dedalus, poking at the dull fire with fierce energy. We're not dead yet, sonny. No, by the Lord Jesus (God forgive me) nor half dead.

Dublin was a new and complex sensation. Uncle Charles had grown so witless that he could no longer be sent out on errands and the disorder in settling in the new house left Stephen freer than he had been in Blackrock. In the beginning he contented himself with circling timidly round the neighbouring square or, at most, going half way down one of the side streets: but when he had made a skeleton map of the city in his mind he followed boldly one of its central lines until he reached the Custom House. He passed unchallenged among the docks and along the quays wondering at the multitude of corks that lay bobbing on the surface of the water in a thick yellow scum, at the crowds of quay porters and the rumbling carts and the illdressed bearded police-man. The vastness and strangeness of the life suggested to him by the bales of merchandise stocked along the walls or swung aloft out of the holds of steamers wakened again in him the un-rest which had sent him wandering in the evening from garden to garden in search of Mercedes. And amid this new bustling life he might have fancied himself in another Marseilles but that he missed the bright sky and the sunwarmed trellisses of the wine-shops. A vague dissatisfaction grew up within him as he looked on the quays and on the river and on the lowering skies and yet he continued to wander up and down day after day as if he really sought someone that eluded him.

He went once or twice with his mother to visit their relatives: and though they passed a jovial array of shops lit up and adorned for Christmas his mood of embittered silence did not leave him. The causes of his embitterment were many, remote and near. He was angry with himself for being young and the prey of restless foolish impulses, angry also with the change of fortune which was reshaping the world about him into a vision of squalor and insincerity. Yet his anger lent nothing to the vision. He chronicled with patience what he saw, detaching himself from it and testing its mortifying flavour in secret.

He was sitting on the backless chair in his aunt's kitchen. A lamp with a reflector hung on the japanned wall of the fireplace and by its light his aunt was reading the evening paper that lay on her knees. She looked a long time at a smiling picture that was set in it and said musingly:

– The beautiful Mabel Hunter!

A ringletted girl stood on tiptoe to peer at the picture and said softly:

– What is she in, mud?[1]

---

[1] an affectionate shortened form for 'mother' (like 'mum')

– In a pantomime, love.

The child leaned her ringletted head against her mother's sleeve, gazing on the picture and murmured as if fascinated:

– The beautiful Mabel Hunter!

As if fascinated, her eyes rested long upon those demurely taunting eyes and she murmured devotedly:

– Isn't she an exquisite creature?

And the boy who came in from the street, stamping crookedly under his stone of coal, heard her words. He dropped his load promptly on the floor and hurried to her side to see. He mauled the edges of the paper with his reddened and blackened hands, shouldering her aside and complaining that he could not see.

He was sitting in the narrow breakfast room high up in the old dark-windowed house. The firelight flickered on the wall and beyond the window a spectral dusk was gathering upon the river. Before the fire an old woman was busy making tea and, as she bustled at the task, she told in a low voice of what the priest and the doctor had said. She told too of certain changes they had seen in her of late and of her odd ways and sayings. He sat listening to the words and following the ways of adventure that lay open in the coals, arches and vaults and winding galleries and jagged caverns.

Suddenly he became aware of something in the doorway. A skull appeared suspended in the gloom of the doorway. A feeble creature like a monkey was there, drawn there by the sound of voices at the fire. A whining voice came from the door asking:

– Is that Josephine?

The old bustling woman answered cheerily from the fireplace:

– No, Ellen, it's Stephen.

– O . . . O, good evening, Stephen.

He answered the greeting and saw a silly smile break over the face in the doorway.

– Do you want anything, Ellen? asked the old woman at the fire.

But she did not answer the question and said:

– I thought it was Josephine. I thought you were Josephine, Stephen.

And, repeating this several times, she fell to laughing feebly.

He was sitting in the midst of a children's party at Harold's Cross. His silent watchful manner had grown upon him and he took little part in the games. The children, wearing the spoils of their crackers, danced and romped noisily and, though he tried to share their merriment, he felt himself a gloomy figure amid the gay cocked hats and sunbonnets.

But when he had sung his song and withdrawn into a snug corner of the room he began to taste the joy of his loneliness. The mirth, which in the beginning of the evening had seemed to him false and trivial, was like a soothing air to him, passing gaily by his senses, hiding from other eyes the feverish agitation of his blood while through the circling of the dancers and amid the music and laughter her glance travelled to his corner, flattering, taunting, searching, exciting his heart.

In the hall the children who had stayed latest were putting on their things: the party was over. She had thrown a shawl about her and, as they went together towards the tram, sprays of her fresh warm breath flew gaily above her cowled head and her shoes tapped blithely on the glassy road.

It was the last tram. The lank brown horses knew it and shook their bells to the clear night in admonition. The conductor talked with the driver, both nodding often in the green light of the lamp. On the empty seats of the tram were scattered a few coloured tickets. No sound of footsteps came up or down the road. No sound broke the peace of the night save when the lank brown horses rubbed their noses together and shook their bells.

They seemed to listen, he on the upper step and she on the lower. She came up to his step many times and went down to hers again between their phrases and once or twice stood close beside him for some moments on the upper step, forgetting to go down, and then went down. His heart danced upon her movements like a cork upon a tide. He heard what her eyes said to him from beneath their cowl and knew that in some dim past, whether in life or reverie, he had heard their tale before. He saw her urge her vanities, her fine dress and sash and long black stockings, and knew that he had yielded to them a thousand times. Yet a voice within him spoke above the noise of his dancing heart, asking him would he take her gift to which he had only to stretch out his hand. And he remembered the day when he and Eileen had stood looking into the hotel grounds, watching the waiters running up a trail of bunting on the flagstaff and the fox terrier scampering to and fro on the sunny lawn, and how, all of a sudden, she had broken out into a peal of laughter and had run down the sloping curve of the path. Now, as then, he stood listlessly in his place, seemingly a tranquil watcher of the scene before him.

– She too wants me to catch hold of her, he thought. That's why she came with me to the tram. I could easily catch hold of her when she comes up to my step: nobody is looking. I could hold her and kiss her.

But he did neither: and, when he was sitting alone in the deserted tram, he tore his ticket into shreds and stared gloomily at the corrugated footboard.

6
Poems from
Chamber Music

i
Strings in the earth and air
    Make music sweet;
Strings by the river where
    The willows meet.

There's music along the river
    For Love wanders there,
Pale flowers on his mantle,
    Dark leaves on his hair.

All softly playing,
    With head to the music bent,
And fingers straying
    Upon an instrument.

ii

The twilight turns from amethyst
 To deep and deeper blue,
The lamp fills with a pale green glow
 The trees of the avenue.

The old piano plays an air,
 Sedate and slow and gay;
She bends upon the yellow keys,
 Her head inclines this way.

Shy thoughts and grave wide eyes and hands
 That wander as they list –
The twilight turns to darker blue
 With lights of amethyst.

v

Lean out of the window,
  Goldenhair,
I heard you singing
  A merry air.

My book is closed;
  I read no more,
Watching the fire dance
  On the floor.

I have left my book:
  I have left my room:
For I heard you singing
  Through the gloom,

Singing and singing
  A merry air.
Lean out of the window,
  Goldenhair.

vii

My love is in a light attire
  Among the apple trees,
Where the gay winds do most desire
  To run in companies.

There, where the gay winds stay to woo
  The young leaves as they pass,
My love goes slowly, bending to
  Her shadow on the grass;

And where the sky's a pale blue cup
  Over the laughing land,
My love goes lightly, holding up
  Her dress with dainty hand.

ix
Winds of May, that dance on the sea,
Dancing a ringaround in glee
From furrow to furrow, while overhead
The foam flies up to be garlanded,
In silvery arches spanning the air,
Saw you my true love anywhere?
   Welladay! Welladay!
   For the winds of May!
Love is unhappy when love is away!

xvii

Because your voice was at my side
　I gave him pain,
Because within my hand I held
　Your hand again.

There is no word nor any sign
　Can make amend –
He is a stranger to me now
　Who was my friend.

XXXV

All day I hear the noise of waters
    Making moan,
Sad as the seabird is when going
    Forth alone
He hears the winds cry to the waters'
    Monotone.

The grey winds, the cold winds are blowing
    Where I go.
I hear the noise of many waters
    Far below.
All day, all night, I hear them flowing
    To and fro.

xxxvi

I hear an army charging upon the land
   And the thunder of horses plunging, foam about their knees
Arrogant, in black armour, behind them stand,
   Disdaining the reins, with fluttering whips, the charioteers.

They cry unto the night their battlename:
   I moan in sleep when I hear afar their whirling laughter.
They cleave the gloom of dreams, a blinding flame,
   Clanging, clanging upon the heart as upon an anvil.

They come shaking in triumph their long green hair:
   They come out of the sea and run shouting by the shore.
My heart, have you no wisdom thus to despair?
   My love, my love, my love, why have you left me alone?

7
The Night of the Whitsuntide Play

The night of the Whitsuntide play had come and Stephen from the window of the dressingroom looked out on the small grass plot across which lines of Chinese lanterns were stretched. He watched the visitors come down the steps from the house and pass into the theatre. Stewards in evening dress, old Belvedereans, loitered in groups about the entrance to the theatre and ushered in the visitors with ceremony. Under the sudden glow of a lantern he could recognize the smiling face of a priest.

The Blessed Sacrament had been removed from the tabernacle and the first benches had been driven back so as to leave the dais of the altar and the space before it free. Against the walls stood companies of barbells[1] and Indian clubs,[1] the dumbbells[1] were piled in one corner: and in the midst of countless hillocks of gymnasium shoes and sweaters and singlets in untidy brown parcels there stood the stout leatherjacketed vaulting horse waiting its turn to be carried up on the stage and set in the middle of the winning team at the end of the gymnastic display.

Stephen, though in deference to his reputation for essay writing he had been elected secretary to the gymnasium,[2] had had no part in the first section of the programme, but in the play which formed the second section he had the chief part, that of a farcical pedagogue. He had been cast for it on account of his stature and grave manners for he was now at the end of his second year at Belvedere and in number two.[3]

A score of the younger boys in white knickers and singlets came pattering down from the stage, through the vestry and into the chapel. The vestry and chapel were peopled with eager masters and boys. The plump bald sergeantmajor was testing with his foot the springboard of the vaulting horse. The lean young man in a long overcoat, who was to give a special display

---

[1] apparatus used in gymnastic exercises

[2] someone responsible for writing up the record of activities of the gymnastic club

[3] the most senior form but one

of intricate club swinging, stood near, watching with interest, his silvercoated clubs peeping out of his deep sidepockets. The hollow rattle of the wooden dumbbells was heard as another team made ready to go up on the stage: and in another moment the excited prefect was hustling the boys through the vestry like a flock of geese, flapping the wings of his soutane nervously and crying to the laggards to make haste. A little troop of Neapolitan peasants were practising their steps at the end of the chapel, some circling their arms above their heads, some swaying their baskets of paper violets and curtsying. In a dark corner of the chapel at the gospel side of the altar[1] a stout old lady knelt amid her copious black skirts. When she stood up a pink-dressed figure, wearing a curly golden wig and an oldfashioned straw sunbonnet, with black pencilled eyebrows and cheeks delicately rouged and powdered, was discovered. A low murmur of curiosity ran round the chapel at the discovery of this girlish figure. One of the prefects, smiling and nodding his head, approached the dark corner and, having bowed to the stout old lady, said pleasantly:

– Is this a beautiful young lady or a doll that you have here, Mrs Tallon?

Then, bending down to peer at the smiling painted face under the leaf of the bonnet, he exclaimed:

– No! Upon my word I believe it's little Bertie Tallon after all!

Stephen at his post by the window heard the old lady and the priest laugh together and heard the boys' murmurs of admiration behind him as they passed forward to see the little boy who had to dance the sunbonnet dance by himself. A movement of impatience escaped him. He let the edge of the blind fall and, stepping down from the bench on which he had been standing, walked out of the chapel.

He passed out of the schoolhouse and halted under the shed that flanked the garden. From the theatre opposite came the muffled noise of the audience and sudden brazen clashes of the soldiers' band. The light spread upwards from the glass roof making the theatre seem a festive ark, anchored among the hulks of houses, her frail cables of lanterns looping her to her moorings. A side door of the theatre opened suddenly and a

---

[1] during the Mass or Communion the reading from the gospels is made from the left-hand side of the altar

shaft of light flew across the grass plots. A sudden burst of music issued from the ark, the prelude of a waltz: and when the side door closed again the listener could hear the faint rhythm of the music. The sentiment of the opening bars, the languor and supple movement, evoked the incommunicable emotion which had been the cause of all his day's unrest and of his impatient movement of a moment before. His unrest issued from him like a wave of sound: and on the tide of flowing music the ark was journeying, trailing her cables of lanterns in her wake. Then a noise like dwarf artillery broke the movement. It was the clapping that greeted the entry of the dumbbell team on the stage.

At the far end of the shed near the street a speck of pink light showed in the darkness and as he walked towards it he became aware of a faint aromatic odour. Two boys were standing in the shelter of a doorway, smoking, and before he reached them he had recognized Heron by his voice.

– Here comes the noble Dedalus! cried a high throaty voice. Welcome to our trusty friend!

This welcome ended in a soft peal of mirthless laughter as Heron salaamed[1] and then began to poke the ground with his cane.

– Here I am, said Stephen, halting and glancing from Heron to his friend.

The latter was a stranger to him but in the darkness, by the aid of the glowing cigarette tips, he could make out a pale dandyish face, over which a smile was travelling slowly, a tall overcoated figure and a hard hat. Heron did not trouble himself about an introduction but said instead:

– I was just telling my friend Wallis what a lark it would be tonight if you took off the rector in the part of the schoolmaster. It would be a ripping good joke.

Heron made a poor attempt to imitate for his friend Wallis the rector's pedantic bass and then, laughing at his failure, asked Stephen to do it.

– Go on, Dedalus, he urged, you can take him off rippingly. *He that will not hear the churcha let him be to theea as the heathena and the publicana.*

The imitation was prevented by a mild expression of anger

---

[1] made the sort of greeting gesture usually employed in the East, chiefly among Muslims

from Wallis in whose mouthpiece the cigarette had become too tightly wedged.

– Damn this blankety blank holder, he said, taking it from his mouth and smiling and frowning upon it tolerantly. It's always getting stuck like that. Do you use a holder?

– I don't smoke, answered Stephen.

– No, said Heron, Dedalus is a model youth. He doesn't smoke and he doesn't go to bazaars and he doesn't flirt and he doesn't damn anything or damn all.

Stephen shook his head and smiled in his rival's flushed and mobile face, beaked like a bird's. He had often thought it strange that Vincent Heron had a bird's face as well as a bird's name. A shock of pale hair lay on the forehead like a ruffled crest: the forehead was narrow and bony and a thin hooked nose stood out between the closeset prominent eyes which were light and inexpressive. The rivals were school friends. They sat together in class, knelt together in the chapel, talked together after beads over their lunches. As the fellows in number one were undistinguished dullards Stephen and Heron had been during the year the virtual heads of the school. It was they who went up to the rector together to ask for a free day or to get a fellow off.

– O, by the way, said Heron suddenly, I saw your governor going in.

The smile waned on Stephen's face. Any allusion made to his father by a fellow or by a master put his calm to rout in a moment. He waited in timorous silence to hear what Heron might say next. Heron, however, nudged him expressively with his elbow and said:

– You're a sly dog.

– Why so? said Stephen.

– You'd think butter wouldn't melt in your mouth, said Heron. But I'm afraid you're a sly dog.

– Might I ask you what you are talking about? said Stephen urbanely.

– Indeed you might, answered Heron. We saw her, Wallis, didn't we? And deucedly pretty she is too. And inquisitive! *And what part does Stephen take, Mr Dedalus? And will Stephen not sing, Mr Dedalus?* Your governor was staring at her through that eyeglass of his for all he was worth so that I think the old man has found you out too. I wouldn't care a bit, by Jove. She's ripping, isn't she, Wallis?

– Not half bad, answered Wallis quietly as he placed his holder once more in a corner of his mouth.

A shaft of momentary anger flew through Stepehen's mind at these indelicate allusions in the hearing of a stranger. For him there was nothing amusing in a girl's interest and regard. All day he had thought of nothing but their leavetaking on the steps of the tram at Harold's Cross, the stream of moody emotions it had made to course through him, and the poem he had written about it. All day he had imagined a new meeting with her for he knew that she was to come to the play. The old restless moodiness had again filled his breast as it has done on the night of the party but had not found an outlet in verse. The growth and knowledge of two years of boyhood stood between then and now, forbidding such an outlet: and all day the stream of gloomy tenderness within him had started forth and returned upon itself in dark courses and eddies, wearying him in the end until the pleasantry of the prefect and the painted little boy had drawn from him a movement of impatience.

– So you may as well admit, Heron went on, that we've fairly found you out this time. You can't play the saint on me any more, that's one sure five.

A soft peal of mirthless laughter escaped from his lips and, bending down as before, he struck Stephen lightly across the calf of the leg with his cane, as if in jesting reproof.

Stephen's movement of anger had already passed. He was neither flattered nor confused, but simply wished the banter to end. He scarcely resented what had seemed to him a silly indelicateness for he knew that the adventure in his mind stood in no danger from these words: and his face mirrored his rival's false smile.

– Admit! repeated Heron, striking him again with his cane across the calf of the leg.

*   *   *   *   *

He remained standing with his two companions at the end of the shed listening idly to their talk or to the bursts of applause in the theatre. She was sitting there among the others perhaps waiting for him to appear. He tried to recall her appearance but could not. He could remember only that she had worn a shawl about her head like a cowl and that her dark eyes had invited and unnerved him. He wondered had he been in her thoughts as

she had been in his. Then in the dark and unseen by the other
two he rested the tips of the fingers of one hand upon the palm
of the other hand, scarcely touching it lightly. But the pressure
of her fingers had been lighter and steadier: and suddenly the
memory of their touch traversed his brain and body like an
invisible wave.

A boy came towards them, running along under the shed. He
was excited and breathless.

– O, Dedalus, he cried, Doyle is in a great bake about you.
You're to go in at once and get dressed for the play. Hurry up,
you better.

– He's coming now, said Heron to the messenger with a
haughty drawl, when he wants to.

The boy turned to Heron and repeated:

– But Doyle is in an awful bake.

– Will you tell Doyle with my best compliments that I
damned his eyes? answered Heron.

– Well, I must go now, said Stephen, who cared little for such
points of honour.

– I wouldn't, said Heron, damn me if I would. That's no way
to send for one of the senior boys. In a bake, indeed! I think it's
quite enough that you're taking a part in his bally old play.

The spirit of quarrelsome comradeship which he had observed
lately in his rival had not seduced Stephen from his habits of
quiet obedience. He mistrusted the turbulence and doubted the
sincerity of such comradeship which seemed to him a sorry
anticipation of manhood. The question of honour here raised
was, like all such questions, trivial to him. While his mind had
been pursuing its intangible phantoms and turning in irre-
solution from such pursuit he had heard about him the constant
voices of his father and of his masters, urging him to be a gentleman above all things and urging him to be a good catholic above
all things. These voices had now come to be hollowsounding in
his ears. When the gymnasium had been opened he had heard
another voice urging him to be strong and manly and healthy
and when the movement towards national revival had begun to
be felt in the college yet another voice had bidden him be true
to his country and help to raise up her language and tradition.
In the profane world, as he foresaw, a worldly voice would bid
him raise up his father's fallen state by his labours and, meanwhile, the voice of his school comrades urged him to be a decent
fellow, to shield others from blame or to beg them off and to do

his best to get free days for the school. And it was the din of all these hollowsounding voices that made him halt irresolutely in the pursuit of phantoms. He gave them ear only for a time but he was happy only when he was far from them, beyond their call, alone or in the company of phantasmal comrades.

In the vestry a plump freshfaced jesuit and an elderly man, in shabby blue clothes, were dabbling in a case of paints and chalks. The boys who had been painted walked about or stood still awkwardly, touching their faces in a gingerly fashion with their furtive fingertips. In the middle of the vestry a young jesuit, who was then on a visit to the college, stood rocking himself rhythmically from the tips of his toes to his heels and back again, his hands thrust well forward into his sidepockets. His small head set off with glossy red curls and his newly shaven face agreed well with the spotless decency of his soutane and with his spotless shoes.

As he watched this swaying form and tried to read for himself the legend of the priest's mocking smile there came into Stephen's memory a saying which he had heard from his father before he had been sent to Clongowes, that you could always tell a jesuit by the style of his clothes. At the same moment he thought he saw a likeness between his father's mind and that of this smiling welldressed priest: and he was aware of some desecration of the priest's office or of the vestry itself whose silence was now routed by loud talk and joking and its air pungent with the smells of the gasjets and the grease.

While his forehead was being wrinkled and his jaws painted black and blue by the elderly man he listened distractedly to the voice of the plump young jesuit which bade him speak up and make his points clearly. He could hear the band playing *The Lily of Killarney*[1] and knew that in a few moments the curtain would go up. He felt no stage fright but the thought of the part he had to play humiliated him. A remembrance of some of his lines made a sudden flush rise to his painted cheeks. He saw her serious alluring eyes watching him from among the audience and their image at once swept away his scruples, leaving his will compact. Another nature seemed to have been lent him: the infection of the excitement and youth about him entered into and transformed his moody mistrustfulness. For one rare moment he seemed to be clothed in the real apparel of boyhood:

[1] a popular song of the time

and, as he stood in the wings among the other players, he shared the common mirth amid which the drop scene was hauled upwards by two ablebodied priests with violent jerks and all awry.

A few moments after he found himself on the stage amid the garish gas and the dim scenery, acting before the innumerable faces of the void. It surprised him to see that the play which he had known at rehearsals for a disjointed lifeless thing had suddenly assumed a life of its own. It seemed now to play itself, he and his fellowactors aiding it with their parts. When the curtain fell on the last scene he heard the void filled with applause and, through a rift in a side scene, saw the simple body before which he had acted magically deformed, the void of faces breaking at all points and falling asunder into busy groups.

He left the stage quickly and rid himself of his mummery and passed out through the chapel into the college garden. Now that the play was over his nerves cried for some further adventure. He hurried onwards as if to overtake it. The doors of the theatre were all open and the audience had emptied out. On the lines which he had fancied the moorings of an ark a few lanterns swung in the night breeze, flickering cheerlessly. He mounted the steps from the garden in haste, eager that some prey should not elude him, and forced his way through the crowd in the hall and past the two jesuits who stood watching the exodus and bowing and shaking hands with the visitors. He pushed onwards nervously feigning a still greater haste and faintly conscious of the smiles and stares and nudges which his powdered head left in its wake.

When he came out on the steps he saw his family waiting for him at the first lamp. In a glance he noted that every figure of the group was familiar and ran down the steps angrily.

– I have to leave a message down in George's Street, he said to his father quickly. I'll be home after you.

Without waiting for his father's questions he ran across the road and began to walk at breakneck speed down the hill. He hardly knew where he was walking. Pride and hope and desire like crushed herbs in his heart sent up vapours of maddening incense before the eyes of his mind. He strode down the hill amid the tumult of suddenrisen vapours of wounded pride and fallen hope and baffled desire. They streamed upwards before his anguished eyes in dense and maddening fumes and passed away above him till at last the air was clear and cold again.

A film still veiled his eyes but they burned no longer. A power, akin to that which had often made anger or resentment fall from him, brought his steps to rest. He stood still and gazed up at the sombre porch of the morgue and from that to the dark cobbled laneway at its side. He saw the word *Lotts* on the wall of the lane and breathed slowly the rank heavy air.

– That is horse piss and rotted straw, he thought. It is a good odour to breathe. It will calm my heart. My heart is quite calm now. I will go back.

Parents

8
A Mother

Mr Holohan, assistant secretary of the *Eire Abu* Society,[1] had been walking up and down Dublin for nearly a month, with his hands and pockets full of dirty pieces of paper, arranging about the series of concerts. He had a game leg, and for this his friends called him Hoppy Holohan. He walked up and down constantly, stood by the hour at street corners arguing the point and made notes; but in the end it was Mrs Kearney who arranged everything.

Miss Devlin had become Mrs Kearney out of spite. She had been educated in a high-class convent, where she had learned French and music. As she was naturally pale and unbending in manner she made few friends at school. When she same to the age of marriage she was sent out to many houses, where her playing and ivory manners were much admired. She sat amid the chilly circle of her accomplishments, waiting for some suitor to brave it and offer her a brilliant life. But the young men whom she met were ordinary and she gave them no encouragement, trying to console her romantic desires by eating a great deal of Turkish Delight in secret. However, when she drew near the limit and her friends began to loosen their tongues about her, she silenced them by marrying Mr Kearney, who was a bootmaker on Ormond Quay.

He was much older than she. His conversation, which was serious, took place at intervals in his great brown beard. After the first year of married life, Mrs Kearney perceived that such a man would wear better than a romantic person, but she never put her own romantic ideas away. He was sober, thrifty and pious; he went to the altar every first Friday, sometimes with her, oftener by himself. But she never weakened in her religion and was a good wife to him. At some party in a strange house when she lifted her eyebrow ever so slightly he stood up to take his leave and, when his cough troubled him, she put the eiderdown quilt over his feet and made a strong rum punch. For his

[1] a society favouring an independent Eire

part, he was a model father. By paying a small sum every week
into a society, he ensured for both his daughters a dowry of one
hundred pounds each when they came to the age of twenty-four.
He sent the older daughter, Kathleen, to a good convent, where
she learned French and music, and afterwards paid her fees at
the Academy. Every year in the month of July Mrs Kearney
found occasion to say to some friend:

'My good man is packing us off to Skerries for a few weeks.'

If it was not Skerries it was Howth or Greystones.[1]

When the Irish Revival began to be appreciable Mrs Kearney
determined to take advantage of her daughter's name and
brought an Irish teacher to the house. Kathleen and her sister
sent Irish picture postcards to their friends and these friends sent
back other Irish picture postcards. On special Sundays, when
Mr Kearney went with his family to the pro-cathedral,[2] a little
crowd of people would assemble after mass at the corner of
Cathedral Street. They were all friends of the Kearneys –
musical friends or Nationalist friends; and, when they had
played every little counter of gossip, they shook hands with one
another all together, laughing at the crossing of so many hands,
and said good-bye to one another in Irish. Soon the name of
Miss Kathleen Kearney began to be heard often on people's lips.
People said that she was very clever at music and a very nice
girl and, moreover, that she was a believer in the language
movement. Mrs Kearney was well content at this. Therefore she
was not surprised when one day Mr Holohan came to her and
proposed that her daughter should be the accompanist at a
series of four grand concerts which his Society was going to give
in the Antient Concert Rooms. She brought him into the
drawing-room, made him sit down and brought out the decanter
and the silver biscuit-barrel. She entered heart and soul into the
details of the enterprise, advised and dissuaded: and finally a
contract was drawn up by which Kathleen was to receive eight
guineas[3] for her services as accompanist at the four grand
concerts.

As Mr Holohan was a novice in such delicate matters as the
wording of bills and the disposing of items for a programme, Mrs

---

[1] holiday resorts

[2] a church used as a cathedral on a temporary basis

[3] in old currency, eight pounds eight shillings (now equivalent to eight pounds
and forty new pence)

Kearney helped him. She had tact. She knew what *artistes* should go into capitals and what *artistes* should go into small type. She knew that the first tenor would not like to come on after Mr Meade's comic turn. To keep the audience continually diverted she slipped the doubtful items in between the old favourites. Mr Holohan called to see her every day to have her advice on some point. She was invariably friendly and advising – homely, in fact. She pushed the decanter towards him, saying:

'Now, help yourself, Mr Holohan!'

And while he was helping himself she said:

'Don't be afraid! Don't be afraid of it!'

Everything went on smoothly. Mrs Kearney bought some lovely blush-pink charmeuse in Brown Thomas's to let into the front of Kathleen's dress. It cost a pretty penny; but there are occasions when a little expense is justifiable. She took a dozen of two-shilling tickets for the final concert and sent them to those friends who could not be trusted to come otherwise. She forgot nothing, and, thanks to her, everything that was to be done was done.

The concerts were to be on Wednesday, Thursday, Friday and Saturday. When Mrs Kearney arrived with her daughter at the Antient Concert Rooms on Wednesday night she did not like the look of things. A few young men, wearing bright blue badges in their coats, stood idle in the vestibule; none of them wore evening dress. She passed by with her daughter and a quick glance through the open door of the hall showed her the cause of the stewards' idleness. At first she wondered had she mistaken the hour. No, it was twenty minutes to eight.

In the dressing-room behind the stage she was introduced to the secretary of the Society, Mr Fitzpatrick. She smiled and shook his hand. He was a little man, with a white, vacant face. She noticed that he wore his soft brown hat carelessly on the side of his head and that his accent was flat. He held a programme in his hand, and, while he was talking to her, he chewed one end of it into a moist pulp. He seemed to bear disappointments lightly. Mr Holohan came into the dressing-room every few minutes with reports from the box-office. The *artistes* talked among themselves nervously, glanced from time to time at the mirror and rolled and unrolled their music. When it was nearly half-past eight, the few people in the hall began to express their desire to be entertained. Mr Fitzpatrick came in, smiled vacantly at the room, and said:

'Well, now, ladies and gentlemen. I suppose we'd better open the ball.'

Mrs Kearney rewarded his very flat final syllable with a quick stare of contempt, and then said to her daughter encouragingly:

'Are you ready, dear?'

When she had an opportunity, she called Mr Holohan aside and asked him to tell her what it meant. Mr Holohan did not know what it meant. He said that the committee had made a mistake in arranging for four concerts: four was too many.

'And the *artistes*!' said Mrs Kearney. 'Of course they are doing their best, but really they are not good.'

Mr Holohan admitted that the *artistes* were no good, but the committee, he said, had decided to let the first three concerts go as they pleased, and reserve all the talent for Saturday night. Mrs Kearney said nothing, but, as the mediocre items followed one another on the platform and the few people in the hall grew fewer and fewer, she began to regret that she had put herself to any expense for such a concert. There was something she didn't like in the look of things and Mr Fitzpatrick's vacant smile irritated her very much. However, she said nothing and waited to see how it would end. The concert expired shortly before ten, and everyone went home quickly.

The concert on Thursday night was better attended, but Mrs Kearney saw at once that the house was filled with paper. The audience behaved indecorously, as if the concert were an informal dress rehearsal. Mr Fitzpatrick seemed to enjoy himself; he was quite unconscious that Mrs Kearney was taking angry note of his conduct. He stood at the edge of the screen, from time to time jutting out his head and exchanging a laugh with two friends in the corner of the balcony. In the course of the evening, Mrs Kearney learned that the Friday concert was to be abandoned and that the committee was going to move heaven and earth to secure a bumper house on Saturday night. When she heard this, she sought out Mr Holohan. She buttonholed him as he was limping out quickly with a glass of lemonade for a young lady and asked him was it true. Yes, it was true.

'But, of course, that doesn't alter the contract,' she said. 'The contract was for four concerts.'

Mr Holohan seemed to be in a hurry; he advised her to speak to Mr Fitzpatrick. Mrs Kearney was now beginning to be alarmed. She called Mr Fitzpatrick away from his screen and told him that her daughter had signed for four concerts and that of course, according to the terms of the contract, she should receive the sum originally stipulated for, whether the society gave the four concerts or not. Mr Fitzpatrick, who did not catch the point at issue very quickly, seemed unable to resolve the difficulty and said that he would bring the matter before the committee. Mrs Kearney's anger began to flutter in her cheek and she had all she could do to keep from asking:

'And who is the *Cometty*[1] pray?'

But she knew that it would not be ladylike to do that: so she was silent.

Little boys were sent out into the principal streets of Dublin early on Friday morning with bundles of handbills. Special puffs[2] appeared in all the evening papers, reminding the music-loving public of the treat which was in store for it on the following evening. Mrs Kearney was somewhat reassured, but she thought well to tell her husband part of her suspicions. He listened carefully and said that perhaps it would be better if he went with her on Saturday night. She agreed. She respected her husband in the same way as she respected the General Post Office, as something large, secure and fixed; and though she knew the small number of his talents she appreciated his abstract value as a male. She was glad that he had suggested coming with her. She thought her plans over.

The night of the grand concert came. Mrs Kearney, with her husband and daughter, arrived at the Antient Concert Rooms three-quarters of an hour before the time at which the concert was to begin. By ill luck it was a rainy evening. Mrs Kearney placed her daughter's clothes and music in charge of her husband and went all over the building looking for Mr Holohan or Mr Fitzpatrick. She could find neither. She asked the stewards was any member of the committee in the hall and, after a great deal of trouble, a steward brought out a little woman named Miss Beirne, to whom Mrs Kearney explained that she wanted to see one of the secretaries. Miss Beirne expected them any minute and asked could she do anything. Mrs Kearney looked searchingly at the oldish face which was screwed into an expression of trustfulness and enthusiasm and answered:

[1] Mrs Kearney's would-be mimicry of Mr Fitzpatrick's pronunciation of 'committee'

[2] advertisements

'No, thank you!'

The little woman hoped they would have a good house. She looked out at the rain until the melancholy of the wet street effaced all the trustfulness and enthusiasm from her twisted features. Then she gave a little sigh and said:

'Ah, well! We did our best, the dear knows.'

Mrs Kearney had to go back to the dressing-room.

The *artistes* were arriving. The bass and the second tenor had already come. The bass, Mr Duggan, was a slender young man with a scattered black moustache. He was the son of a hall porter in an office in the city and, as a boy, he had sung prolonged bass notes in the resounding hall. From this humble state he had raised himself until he had become a first-rate *artiste*. He had appeared in grand opera. One night, when an operatic *artiste* had fallen ill, he had undertaken the part of the king in the opera of *Maritana* at the Queen's Theatre. He sang his music with great feeling and volume and was warmly welcomed by the gallery; but, unfortunately, he marred the good impression by wiping his nose in his gloved hand once or twice out of thoughtlessness. He was unassuming and spoke little. He said *yous* so softly that it passed unnoticed and he never drank anything stronger than milk for his voice's sake. Mr Bell, the second tenor, was a fair-haired little man who competed every year for prizes at the Feis Ceoil.[1] On his fourth trial he had been awarded a bronze medal. He was extremely nervous and extremely jealous of other tenors and he covered his nervous jealousy with an ebullient friendliness. It was his humour to have people know what an ordeal a concert was to him. Therefore when he saw Mr Duggan he went over to him and asked:

'Are you in it too?'

'Yes,' said Mr Duggan.

Mr Bell laughed at his fellow-sufferer, held out his hand and said:

'Shake!'

Mrs Kearney passed by these two young men and went to the edge of the screen to view the house. The seats were being filled up rapidly and a pleasant noise circulated in the auditorium. She came back and spoke to her husband privately. Their conversation was evidently about Kathleen for they both glanced at her often as she stood chatting to one of her Nationalist

[1] Irish national music competition, held annually, usually in Dublin

friends, Miss Healy, the contralto. An unknown solitary woman with a pale face walked through the room. The women followed with keen eyes the faded blue dress which was stretched upon a meagre body. Someone said that she was Madam Glynn, the soprano.

'I wonder where did they dig her up,' said Kathleen to Miss Healy. 'I'm sure I never heard of her.'

Miss Healy had to smile. Mr Holohan limped into the dressing-room at that moment and the two young ladies asked him who was the unknown woman. Mr Holohan said that she was Madam Glynn from London. Madam Glynn took her stand in a corner of the room, holding a roll of music stiffly before her and from time to time changing the direction of her startled gaze. The shadow took her faded dress into shelter but fell revengefully into the little cup behind her collar-bone. The noise of the hall became more audible. The first tenor and the baritone arrived together. They were both well dressed, stout and complacent and they brought a breath of opulence among the company.

Mrs Kearney brought her daughter over to them, and talked to them amiably. She wanted to be on good terms with them but, while she strove to be polite, her eyes followed Mr Holohan in his limping and devious courses. As soon as she could she excused herself and went out after him.

'Mr Holohan, I want to speak to you for a moment,' she said.

They went down to a discreet part of the corridor. Mrs Kearney asked him when was her daughter going to be paid. Mr Holohan said that Mr Fitzpatrick had charge of that. Mrs Kearney said that she didn't know anything about Mr Fitzpatrick. Her daughter had signed a contract for eight guineas, and she would have to be paid. Mr Holohan said that it wasn't his business.

'Why isn't it your business?' asked Mrs Kearney. 'Didn't you yourself bring her the contract? Anyway, if it's not your business it's my business and I mean to see to it.'

'You'd better speak to Mr Fitzpatrick,' said Mr Holohan distantly.

'I don't know anything about Mr Fitzpatrick,' repeated Mrs Kearney. 'I have my contract, and I intend to see that it is carried out.'

When she came back to the dressing-room her cheeks were slightly suffused. The room was lively. Two men in outdoor dress had taken possession of the fireplace and were chatting familiarly with Miss Healy and the baritone. They were the *Freeman* man and Mr O'Madden Burke. The *Freeman* man had come in to say that he could not wait for the concert as he had to report the lecture which an American priest was giving in the Mansion House. He said they were to leave the report for him at the *Freeman* office and he would see that it went in. He was a grey-haired man, with a plausible voice and careful manners. He held an extinguished cigar in his hand and the aroma of cigar smoke floated near him. He had not intended to stay a moment because concerts and *artistes* bored him considerably, but he remained leaning against the mantelpiece. Miss Healy stood in front of him, talking and laughing. He was old enough to suspect one reason for her politeness, but young enough in spirit to turn the moment to account. The warmth, fragrance and colour of her body appealed to his senses. He was pleasantly conscious that the bosom which he saw rise and fall slowly beneath him rose and fell at that moment for him, that the laughter and fragrance and wilful glances were his tribute. When he could stay no longer he took leave of her regretfully.

O'Madden Burke will write the notice,' he explained to Mr Holohan, 'and I'll see it in.'

'Thank you very much, Mr Hendrick,' said Mr Holohan. 'You'll see it in, I know. Now, won't you have a little something before you go?'

'I don't mind,' said Mr Hendrick.

The two men went along some tortuous passages and up a dark staircase and came to a secluded room where one of the stewards was uncorking bottles for a few gentlemen. One of these gentlemen was Mr O'Madden Burke, who had found out the room by instinct. He was a suave, elderly man who balanced his imposing body, when at rest, upon a large silk umbrella. His magniloquent western name was the moral umbrella upon which he balanced the fine problem of his finances. He was widely respected.

While Mr Holohan was entertaining the *Freeman* man Mrs Kearney was speaking so animatedly to her husband that he had to ask her to lower her voice. The conversation of the others in the dressing-room had become strained. Mr Bell, the first item, stood ready with his music, but the accompanist made no sign. Evidently something was wrong. Mr Kearney looked straight before him, stroking his beard, while Mrs Kearney spoke into

Kathleen's ear with subdued emphasis. From the hall came sounds of encouragement, clapping and stamping of feet. The first tenor and the baritone and Miss Healy stood together, waiting tranquilly, but Mr Bell's nerves were greatly agitated because he was afraid the audience would think that he had come late.

Mr Holohan and Mr O'Madden Burke came into the room. In a moment Mr Holohan perceived the hush. He went over to Mrs Kearney and spoke with her earnestly. While they were speaking the noise in the hall grew louder. Mr Holohan became very red and excited. He spoke volubly, but Mrs Kearney said curtly at intervals:

'She won't go on. She must get her eight guineas.'

Mr Holohan pointed desperately towards the hall where the audience was clapping and stamping. He appealed to Mr Kearney and to Kathleen. But Mr Kearney continued to stroke his beard and Kathleen looked down moving the point of her new shoe: it was not her fault. Mrs Kearney repeated:

'She won't go on without her money.'

After a swift struggle of tongues Mr Holohan hobbled out in haste. The room was silent. When the strain of the silence had become somewhat painful Miss Healy said to the baritone:

'Have you seen Mrs Pat Campbell this week?'

The baritone had not seen her but he had been told that she was very fine. The conversation went no further. The first tenor bent his head and began to count the links of the gold chain which was extended across his waist, smiling and humming random notes to observe the effect on the frontal sinus. From time to time everyone glanced at Mrs Kearney.

The noise in the auditorium had risen to a clamour when Mr Fitzpatrick burst into the room, followed by Mr Holohan, who was panting. The clapping and stamping in the hall were punctuated by whistling. Mr Fitzpatrick held a few bank notes in his hand. He counted out four into Mrs Kearney's hand and said she would get the other half at the interval. Mrs Kearney said:

'This is four shillings short.'

But Kathleen gathered in her skirt and said: '*Now. Mr Bell.*' to the first item, who was shaking like an aspen. The singer and the accompanist went out together. The noise in the hall died away. There was a pause of a few seconds: and then the piano was heard.

The first part of the concert was very successful except for Madam Glynn's item. The poor lady sang *Killarney* in a bodiless gasping voice, with all the old-fashioned mannerisms of intonation and pronunciation which she believed lent elegance to her singing. She looked as if she had been resurrected from an old stage wardrobe and the cheaper parts of the hall made fun of her high wailing notes. The first tenor and the contralto, however, brought down the house. Kathleen played a selection of Irish airs which was generously applauded. The first part closed with a stirring patriotic recitation delivered by a young lady who arranged amateur theatricals. It was deservedly applauded; and, when it was ended, the men went out for the interval, content.

All this time the dressing-room was a hive of excitement. In one corner were Mr Holohan, Mr Fitzpatrick, Miss Beirne, two of the stewards, the baritone, the bass, and Mr O'Madden Burke. Mr O'Madden Burke said it was the most scandalous exhibition he had ever witnessed. Miss Kathleen Kearney's musical career was ended in Dublin after that, he said. The baritone was asked what did he think of Mrs Kearney's conduct. He did not like to say anything. He had been paid his money and wished to be at peace with men. However, he said that Mrs Kearney might have taken the *artistes* into consideration. The stewards and the secretaries debated hotly as to what should be done when the interval came.

'I agree with Miss Beirne,' said Mr O'Madden Burke. 'Pay her nothing.'

In another corner of the room were Mrs Kearney and her husband, Mr Bell, Miss Healy and the young lady who had to recite the patriotic piece. Mrs Kearney said that the committee had treated her scandalously. She had spared neither trouble nor expense and this was how she was repaid.

They thought they had only a girl to deal with and that, therefore, they could ride roughshod over her. But she would show them their mistake. They wouldn't have dared to have treated her like that if she had been a man. But she would see that her daughter got her rights: she wouldn't be fooled. If they didn't pay her to the last farthing[1] she would make Dublin ring. Of course she was sorry for the sake of the *artistes*. But what else could she do? She appealed to the second tenor, who said he

---

[1] quarter of an old penny

thought she had not been well treated. Then she appealed to Miss Healy. Miss Healy wanted to join the other group, but she did not like to do so because she was a great friend of Kathleen's and the Kearneys had often invited her to their house.

As soon as the first part was ended Mr Fitzpatrick and Mr Holohan went over to Mrs Kearney and told her that the other four guineas would be paid after the committee meeting on the following Thursday and that, in case her daughter did not play for the second part, the committee would consider the contract broken and would pay nothing.

'I haven't seen any committee,' said Mrs Kearney angrily. 'My daughter has her contract. She will get four pounds eight into her hand or a foot she won't put on that platform.'

'I'm surprised at you, Mrs Kearney,' said Mr Holohan. 'I never throught you would treat us this way.'

'And what way did you treat me?' asked Mrs Kearney.

Her face was inundated with an angry colour and she looked as if she would attack someone with her hands.

'I'm asking for my rights,' she said.

'You might have some sense of decency,' said Mr Holohan.

'Might I, indeed? . . . And when I ask when my daughter is going to be paid I can't get a civil answer.'

She tossed her head and assumed a haughty voice:

'You must speak to the secretary. It's not my business. I'm a great fellow fol-the-diddle-I-do.'

'I thought you were a lady,' said Mr Holohan, walking away from her abruptly.

After that Mrs Kearney's conduct was condemned on all hands: everyone approved of what the committee had done. She stood at the door, haggard with rage, arguing with her husband and daughter, gesticulating with them. She waited until it was time for the second part to begin in the hope that the secretaries would approach her. But Miss Healy had kindly consented to play one or two accompaniments. Mrs Kearney had to stand aside to allow the baritone and his accompanist to pass up to the platform. She stood still for an instant like an angry stone image and, when the first notes of the song struck her ear, she caught up her daughter's cloak and said to her husband:

'Get a cab!'

He went out at once. Mrs Kearney wrapped the cloak round her daughter and followed him. As she passed through the doorway she stopped and glared into Mr Holohan's face.

'I'm not done with you, yet,' she said.

'But I've done with you,' said Mr Holohan.

Kathleen followed her mother meekly. Mr Holohan began to pace up and down the room, in order to cool himself for he felt his skin on fire.

'That's a nice lady!' he said. 'O, she's a nice lady!'

'You did the proper thing, Holohan,' said Mr O'Madden Burke, poised upon his umbrella in approval.

9
Poems from Pomes Penyeach

Frail the white rose and frail are
Her hand that gave
Whose soul is sere[1] and paler
Than time's wan[2] wave.

Rosefrail and fair – yet frailest
A wonder wild
In gentle eyes thou veilest,
My blueveined child.

[1] withered and dried up
[2] pale, drained of blood

ON THE BEACH AT FONTANA

Wind whines and whines the shingle,
The crazy pierstakes groan;
A senile sea numbers each single
Slimesilvered stone.

From whining wind and colder
Grey sea I wrap him warm
And touch his trembling fineboned shoulder
And boyish arm.

Around us fear, descending
Darkness of fear above
And in my heart how deep unending
Ache of love!

10
A Trip to Cork

Stephen was once again seated beside his father in the corner of a railway carriage at King's Bridge. He was travelling with his father by the night mail to Cork. As the train steamed out of the station he recalled his childish wonder of years before and every event of his first day at Clongowes. But he felt no wonder now. He saw the darkening lands slipping away past him, the silent telegraphpoles passing his window swiftly every four seconds, the little glimmering stations, manned by a few silent sentries, flung by the mail behind her and twinkling for a moment in the darkness like fiery grains flung backwards by a runner.

He listened without sympathy to his father's evocation of Cork and of scenes of his youth – a tale broken by sighs or draughts from his pocket flask whenever the image of some dead friend appeared in it, or whenever the evoker remembered suddenly the purpose of his actual visit. Stephen heard, but could feel no pity. The images of the dead were all strangers to him save that of uncle Charles, an image which had lately been fading out of memory. He knew, however, that his father's property was going to be sold by auction and in the manner of his own dispossession he felt the world give the lie rudely to his phantasy.

At Maryborough he fell asleep. When he awoke the train had passed out of Mallow and his father was stretched asleep on the other seat. The cold light of the dawn lay over the country, over the unpeopled fields and the closed cottages. The terror of sleep fascinated his mind as he watched the silent country or heard from time to time his father's deep breath or sudden sleepy movement. The neighbourhood of unseen sleepers filled him with strange dread, as though they could harm him, and he prayed that the day might come quickly. His prayer, addressed neither to God nor saint, began with a shiver, as the chilly morning breeze crept through the chink of the carriage door to his feet, and ended in a trail of foolish words which he made to fit the insistent rhythm of the train; and silently, at intervals of four seconds, the telegraphpoles held the galloping notes of the music between punctuated bars. This furious music allayed his dread and, leaning against the windowledge, he let his eyelids close again.

They drove in a jingle across Cork while it was still early morning and Stephen finished his sleep in a bedroom of the Victoria Hotel. The bright warm sunlight was streaming through the window and he could hear the din of traffic. His father was standing before the dressingtable, examining his hair and face and moustache with great care, craning his neck across the waterjug and drawing it back sideways to see the better. While he did so he sang softly to himself with quaint accent and phrasing:

> 'Tis youth and folly
> Makes young men marry,
> So here, my love, I'll
>   No longer stay.
> What can't be cured, sure,
> Must be injured, sure,
>   So I'll go to
>   Amerikay.
>
> My love she's handsome,
> My love she's bony:
> She's like good whisky
>   When it is new;
> But when 'tis old
> And growing cold
> It fades and dies like
>   The mountain dew.

The consciousness of the warm sunny city outside his window and the tender tremors with which his father's voice festooned the strange sad happy air, drove off all the mists of the night's ill humour from Stephen's brain. He got up quickly to dress and, when the song had ended, said:

– That's much prettier than any of your other *come-all-yous*.

– Do you think so? asked Mr Dedalus.

– I like it, said Stephen.

– It's a pretty old air, said Mr Dedalus, twirling the points of his moustache. Ah, but you should have heard Mick Lacy sing it! Poor Mick Lacy! He had little turns for it, grace notes he used to put in that I haven't got. That was the boy who could sing a *come-all-you*, if you like.

Mr Dedalus had ordered drisheens for breakfast and during the meal he crossexamined the waiter for local news. For the most part they spoke at cross purposes when a name was mentioned, the waiter having in mind the present holder and Mr Dedalus his father or perhaps his grandfather.

– Well, I hope they haven't moved the Queen's College anyhow, said Mr Dedalus, for I want to show it to this youngster of mine.

Along the Mardyke the trees were in bloom. They entered the grounds of the college and were led by the garrulous porter across the quadrangle. But their progress across the gravel was brought to a halt after every dozen or so paces by some reply of the porter's.

– Ah, do you tell me so? And is poor Pottlebelly dead?

– Yes, sir. Dead, sir.

During these halts Stephen stood awkwardly behind the two men, weary of the subject and waiting restlessly for the slow march to begin again. By the time they had crossed the quadrangle his restlessness had risen to fever. He wondered how his father, whom he knew for a shrewd suspicious man, could be duped by the servile manners of the porter; and the lively southern speech which had entertained him all the morning now irritated his ears.

They passed into the anatomy theatre where Mr Dedalus, the porter aiding him, searched the desks for his initials. Stephen remained in the background, depressed more than ever by the darkness and silence of the theatre and by the air it wore of jaded and formal study. On the desk he read the word *Foetus*[1] cut several times in the dark stained wood. The sudden legend startled his blood: he seemed to feel the absent students of the college about him and to shrink from their company. A vision of their life, which his father's words had been powerless to evoke, sprang up before him out of the word cut in the desk. A broad-shouldered student with a moustache was cutting in the letters with a jack knife, seriously. Other students stood or sat near him laughing at his handiwork. One jogged his elbow. The big

[1] the young animal still in the womb or egg, but after its parts have been distinctly formed

student turned on him, frowning. He was dressed in loose grey clothes and had tan boots.

Stephen's name was called. He hurried down the steps of the theatre so as to be as far away from the vision as he could be and, peering closely at his father's initials, hid his flushed face.

But the word and the vision capered before his eyes as he walked back across the quadrangle and towards the college gate. It shocked him to find in the outer world a trace of what he had deemed till then a brutish and individual malady of his own mind. His monstrous reveries came thronging into his memory. They too had sprung up before him, suddenly and furiously, out of mere words. He had soon given in to them, and allowed them to sweep across and abase his intellect, wondering always where they came from, from what den of monstrous images, and always weak and humble towards others, restless and sickened of himself when they had swept over him.

– Ay, bedad! And there's the Groceries sure enough! cried Mr Dedalus. You often heard me speak of the Groceries, didn't you, Stephen? Many's the time we went down there when our names had been marked, a crowd of us, Harry Peard and little Jack Mountain and Bob Dyas and Maurice Moriarty, the Frenchman, and Tom O'Grady and Mick Lacy that I told you of this morning and Joey Corbet and poor little goodhearted Johnny Keevers of the Tantiles.

The leaves of the trees along the Mardyke were astir and whispering in the sunlight. A team of cricketers passed, agile young men in flannels and blazers, one of them carrying the long green wicketbag. In a quiet bystreet a German band of five players in faded uniforms and with battered brass instruments was playing to an audience of street arabs and leisurely messenger boys. A maid in a white cap and apron was watering a box of plants on a sill which shone like a slab of limestone in the warm glare. From another window open to the air came the sound of a piano, scale after scale rising into the treble.

Stephen walked on at his father's side, listening to stories he had heard before, hearing again the names of the scattered and dead revellers who had been the companions of his father's youth. And a faint sickness sighed in his heart. He recalled his own equivocal position in Belvedere, a free boy, a leader afraid of his own authority, proud and sensitive and suspicious, battling against the squalor of his life and against the riot of his mind. The letters cut in the stained wood of the desk stared

upon him, mocking his bodily weakness and futile enthusiasms
and making him loathe himself for his own mad and filthy
orgies. The spittle in this throat grew bitter and foul to swallow
and the faint sickness climbed to his brain so that for a moment
he closed his eyes and walked on in darkness.

He could still hear his father's voice –

– When you kick out for yourself, Stephen – as I daresay you
will one of these days – remember, whatever you do, to mix
with gentlemen. When I was a young fellow I tell you I enjoyed myself. I mixed with fine decent fellows. Everyone of us
could do something. One fellow had a good voice, another
fellow was a good actor, another could sing a good comic song,
another was a good oarsman or a good racket player, another
could tell a good story and so on. We kept the ball rolling anyhow and enjoyed ourselves and saw a bit of life and we were
none the worse of it either. But we were all gentlemen, Stephen
– at least I hope we were – and bloody good honest Irishmen
too. That's the kind of fellows I want you to associate with,
fellows of the right kidney. I'm talking to you as a friend,
Stephen. I don't believe a son should be afraid of his father. No,
I treat you as your grandfather treated me when I was a young
chap. We were more like brothers than father and son. I'll
never forget the first day he caught me smoking. I was standing
at the end of the South Terrace one day with some maneens[1]
like myself and sure we thought we were grand fellows because
we had pipes stuck in the corners of our mouths. Suddenly the
governor passed. He didn't say a word, or stop even. But the
next day, Sunday, we were out for a walk together and when
we were coming home he took out his cigar case and said: – By
the by, Simon, I didn't know you smoked, or something like
that. – Of course I tried to carry it off as best I could. – If you
want a good smoke, he said, try one of these cigars. An American
captain made me a present of them last night in Queenstown.

Stephen heard his father's voice break into a laugh which was
almost a sob.

– He was the handsomest man in Cork at that time, by God
he was! The women used to stand to look after him in the street.

He heard the sob passing loudly down his father's throat and
opened his eyes with a nervous impulse. The sunlight breaking
suddenly on his sight turned the sky and clouds into a fantastic

[1] young men

world of sombre masses with lakelike spaces of dark rosy light. His very brain was sick and powerless. He could scarcely interpret the letters of the signboards of the shops. By his monstrous way of life he seemed to have put himself beyond the limits of reality. Nothing moved him or spoke to him from the real world unless he heard in it an echo of the infuriated cries within him. He could respond to no earthly or human appeal, dumb and insensible to the call of summer and gladness and companionship, wearied and dejected by his father's voice. He could scarcely recognize as his his own thoughts, and repeated slowly to himself:

– I am Stephen Dedalus. I am walking beside my father whose name is Simon Dedalus. We are in Cork, in Ireland. Cork is a city. Our room is in the Victoria Hotel. Victoria and Stephen and Simon. Simon and Stephen and Victoria. Names.

The memory of his childhood suddenly grew dim. He tried to call forth some of its vivid moments but could not. He recalled only names. Dante,[1] Parnell,[2] Clane,[3] Clongowes. A little boy had been taught geography by an old woman who kept two brushes in her wardrobe. Then he had been sent away from home to a college, he had made his first communion and eaten slim jim[4] out of his cricket cap and watched the firelight leaping and dancing on the wall of a little bedroom in the infirmary and dreamed of being dead, of mass being said for him by the rector in a black and gold cope, of being buried then in the little grave-yard of the community off the main avenue of limes. But he had not died then. Parnell had died. There had been no mass for the dead in the chapel, and no procession. He had not died but he had faded out like a film in the sun. He had been lost or had wandered out of existence for he no longer existed. How strange to think of him passing out of existence in such a way, not by death, but by fading out in the sun or by being lost and forgotten somewhere in the universe! It was strange to see his small body appear again for a moment: a little boy in a grey belted suit. His

---

[1] Mrs 'Dante' Hearn Conway was a woman who lived with the Joyce family during James's early years. She taught him reading, writing, arithmetic and geography and is referred to simply as 'Dante' in *Portrait of the Artist*

[2] Charles Parnell was an Irish politician and leading nationalist who had been the centre of a public scandal during the years of James's childhood

[3] the town near which Clongowes Wood College was situated

[4] a sort of plain cake

hands were in his sidepockets and his trousers were tucked in at the knees by elastic bands.

On the evening of the day on which the property was sold Stephen followed his father meekly about the city from bar to bar. To the sellers in the market, to the barmen and barmaids, to the beggars who importuned him for a lob[1] Mr Dedalus told the same tale, that he was an old Corkonian, that he had been trying for thirty years to get rid of his Cork accent up in Dublin and that Peter Pickackafax beside him was his eldest son but that he was only a Dublin jackeen.[2]

They had set out early in the morning from Newcombe's coffee-house, where Mr Dedalus's cup had rattled noisily against its saucer, and Stephen had tried to cover that shameful sign of his father's drinkingbout of the night before by moving his chair and coughing. One humiliation had succeeded another – the false smiles of the market sellers, the curvetings[3] and oglings of the barmaids with whom his father flirted, the compliments and encouraging words of his father's friends. They had told him that he had a great look of his grandfather and Mr Dedalus had agreed that he was an ugly likeness. They had unearthed traces of a Cork accent in his speech and made him admit that the Lee[4] was a much finer river than the Liffey.[5] One of them, in order to put his Latin to the proof, had made him translate short passages from Dilectus, and asked him whether it was correct to say: *Tempora mutantur nos et mutamur in illis,* or *Tempora mutantur et nos mutamur in illis.*[6] Another, a brisk old man, whom Mr Dedalus called Johnny Cashman, had covered him with confusion by asking him to say which were prettier, the Dublin girls or the Cork girls.

– He's not that way built, said Mr Dedalus. Leave him alone. He's a levelheaded thinking boy who doesn't bother his head about that kind of nonsense.

– Then he's not his father's son, said the little old man.

[1] gift of a few coins

[2] young fellow

[3] friskings, cavortings

[4] the river on which Cork stands

[5] one of the rivers of Dublin

[6] Both versions of this Latin tag mean 'Times change and we change with them', though the former is thought to be the more 'correct'

— I don't know, I'm sure, said Mr Dedalus, smiling complacently.

— Your father, said the little old man to Stephen, was the boldest flirt in the city of Cork in his day. Do you know that?

Stephen looked down and studied the tiled floor of the bar into which they had drifted.

— Now don't be putting ideas into his head, said Mr Dedalus. Leave him to his Maker.

— Yerra, sure I wouldn't put any ideas into his head. I'm old enough to be his grandfather. And I am a grandfather, said the little old man to Stephen. Do you know that?

— Are you? asked Stephen.

— Bedad I am, said the little old man. I have two bouncing grandchildren out at Sunday's Well. Now, then! What age do you think I am? And I remember seeing your grandfather in his red coat riding out to hounds. That was before you were born.

— Ay, or thought of, said Mr Dedalus.

— Bedad I did, repeated the little old man. And, more than that, I can remember even your grandfather, old John Stephen Dedalus, and a fierce old fireeater he was. Now, then! There's a memory for you!

— That's three generations – four generations, said another of the company. Why, Johnny Cashman, you must be nearing the century.

— Well, I'll tell you the truth, said the little old man. I'm just twenty-seven years of age.

— We're as old as we feel, Johnny, said Mr Dedalus. And just finish what you have there, and we'll have another. Here, Tim or Tom or whatever your name is, give us the same again here. By God, I don't feel more than eighteen myself. There's that son of mine there not half my age and I'm a better man than he is any day of the week.

— Draw it mild now, Dedalus. I think it's time for you to take a back seat, said the gentleman who had spoken before.

— No, by God! asserted Mr Dedalus. I'll sing a tenor song against him or I'll vault a fivebarred gate against him or I'll run with him after the hounds across the country as I did thirty years ago along with the Kerry Boy and the best man for it.

— But he'll beat you here, said the little old man, tapping his forehead and raising his glass to drain it.

— Well, I hope he'll be as good a man as his father. That's all I can say, said Mr Dedalus.

– If he is, he'll do, said the little old man.

– And thanks be to God, Johnny, said Mr Dedalus, that we lived so long and did so little harm.

– But did so much good, Simon, said the little old man gravely. Thanks be to God we lived so long and did so much good.

Stephen watched the three glasses being raised from the counter as his father and his two cronies drank to the memory of their past. An abyss of fortune or of temperament sundered him from them. His mind seemed older than theirs: it shone coldly on their strifes and happiness and regrets like a moon upon a younger earth.

On Our Own

11
After the Race

The cars came scudding in towards Dublin, running evenly like pellets in the groove of the Naas Road. At the crest of the hill at Inchicore sightseers had gathered in clumps to watch the cars careering homeward, and through this channel of poverty and inaction the Continent sped its wealth and industry. Now and again the clumps of people raised the cheer of the gratefully oppressed. Their sympathy, however, was for the blue cars – the cars of their friends, the French.

The French, moreover, were virtual victors. Their team had finished solidly; they had been placed second and third and the driver of the winning German car was reported a Belgian. Each blue car, therefore, received a double measure of welcome as it topped the crest of the hill, and each cheer of welcome was acknowledged with smiles and nods by those in the car. In one of these trimly built cars was a party of four young men whose spirits seemed to be at present well above the level of successful Gallicism: in fact, these four young men were almost hilarious. They were Charles Ségouin, the owner of the car; André Rivière, a young electrician of Canadian birth; a huge Hungarian named Villona and a neatly groomed young man named Doyle. Ségouin was in good humour because he had unexpectedly received some orders in advance (he was about to start a motor establishment in Paris) and Rivière was in good humour because he was to be appointed manager of the establishment; these two young men (who were cousins) were also in good humour because of the success of the French cars. Villona was in good humour because he had had a very satisfactory luncheon; and, besides, he was an optimist by nature. The fourth member of the party, however, was too excited to be genuinely happy.

He was about twenty-six years of age, with a soft, light-brown moustache and rather innocent-looking grey eyes. His father, who had begun life as an advanced Nationalist, had modified his views early. He had made his money as a butcher in Kingstown and by opening shops in Dublin and in the suburbs he had made his money many times over. He had also been fortunate enough to secure some of the police contracts and in the end he had become rich enough to be alluded to in the Dublin newspapers as a merchant prince. He had sent his son to England to be educated in a big Catholic college and had afterwards sent him to Dublin University to study law. Jimmy did not study very earnestly and took to bad courses for a while. He had money and he was popular; and he divided his time curiously between musical and motoring circles. Then he had been sent for a term to Cambridge to see a little life. His father, remonstrative, but covertly proud of the excess, had paid his bills and brought him home. It was at Cambridge that he had met Ségouin. They were not much more than acquaintances as yet, but Jimmy found great pleasure in the society of one who had seen so much of the world and was reputed to own some of the biggest hotels in France. Such a person (as his father agreed) was well worth knowing, even if he had not been the charming companion he was. Villona was entertaining also – a brilliant pianist – but, unfortunately, very poor.

The car ran on merrily with its cargo of hilarious youth. The two cousins sat on the front seat; Jimmy and his Hungarian friend sat behind. Decidedly Villona was in excellent spirits; he kept up a deep bass hum of melody for miles of the road. The Frenchmen flung their laughter and light words over their shoulders, and often Jimmy had to strain forward to catch the quick phrase. This was not altogether pleasant for him, as he had nearly always to make a deft guess at the meaning and shout back a suitable answer in the face of a high wind. Besides, Villona's humming would confuse anybody; the noise of the car, too.

Rapid motion through space elates one; so does notoriety; so does the possession of money. These were three good reasons for Jimmy's excitement. He had been seen by many of his friends that day in the company of these Continentals. At the control Ségouin had presented him to one of the French competitors and, in answer to his confused murmur of compliment, the swarthy face of the driver had disclosed a line of shining white teeth. It was pleasant after that honour to return to the profane world of spectators amid nudges and significant looks. Then as to money – he really had a great sum under his control. Ségouin, perhaps, would not think it a great sum, but Jimmy who, in spite of temporary errors, was at heart the inheritor of solid instincts knew well with what difficulty it had been got together. This knowledge had previously kept his bills within the limits of reasonable recklessness, and if he had been so conscious of the labour latent in money when there had been question merely of some freak of the higher intelligence, how much more so now when he was about to stake the greater part of his substance! It was a serious thing for him.

Of course, the investment was a good one, and Ségouin had managed to give the impression that it was by a favour of friendship the mite of Irish money was to be included in the capital of the concern. Jimmy had a respect for his father's shrewdness in business matters, and in this case it had been his father who had first suggested the investment; money to be made in the motor business, pots of money. Moreover, Ségouin had the unmistakable air of wealth. Jimmy set out to translate into days' work that lordly car in which he sat. How smoothly it ran! In what style they had come careering along the country roads! The journey laid a magical finger on the genuine pulse of life and gallantly the machinery of human nerves strove to answer the bounding courses of the swift blue animal.

They drove down Dame Street. The street was busy with unusual traffic, loud with the horns of motorists and the gongs of impatient tram-drivers. Near the Bank Ségouin drew up and Jimmy and his friend alighted. A little knot of people collected on the footpath to pay homage to the snorting motor. The party was to dine together that evening in Ségouin's hotel and, meanwhile, Jimmy and his friend, who was staying with him, were to go home to dress. The car steered out slowly for Grafton Street while the two young men pushed their way through the knot of gazers. They walked northward with a curious feeling of disappointment in the exercise, while the city hung its pale globes of light above them in a haze of summer evening.

In Jimmy's house this dinner had been pronounced an occasion. A certain pride mingled with his parents' trepidation, a certain eagerness, also, to play fast and loose for the names of great foreign cities have at least this virtue. Jimmy, too, looked very well when he was dressed and, as he stood in the hall, giving a last equation to the bows of his dress tie, his father may have felt even commercially satisfied at having secured for his son qualities often unpurchasable. His father, therefore, was unusually friendly with Villona, and his manner expressed a real respect for foreign accomplishments; but this subtlety of his host was probably lost upon the Hungarian, who was beginning to have a sharp desire for his dinner.

The dinner was excellent, exquisite. Ségouin, Jimmy decided, had a very refined taste. The party was increased by a young Englishman named Routh whom Jimmy had seen with Ségouin at Cambridge. The young men supped in a snug room lit by electric candle lamps. They talked volubly and with little reserve. Jimmy, whose imagination was kindling, conceived the lively youth of the Frenchmen twined elegantly upon the firm framework of the Englishman's manner. A graceful image of his, he thought, and a just one. He admired the dexterity with which their host directed the conversation. The five young men had various tastes and their tongues had been loosened. Villona, with immense respect, began to discover to the mildly surprised Englishman the beauties of the English madrigal, deploring the loss of old instruments. Rivière, not wholly ingenuously, undertook to explain to Jimmy the triumph of the French mechanicians. The resonant voice of the Hungarian was about to prevail in ridicule of the spurious lutes of the romantic painters when Ségouin shepherded his party into politics. Here was congenial ground for all. Jimmy, under generous influences, felt the buried zeal of his father wake to life within him: he aroused the torpid Routh at last. The room grew doubly hot and Ségouin's task grew harder each moment: there was even danger of personal spite. The alert host at an opportunity lifted his glass to Humanity, and when the toast had been drunk he threw open a window significantly.

That night the city wore the mask of a capital. The five young men strolled along Stephen's Green in a faint cloud of aromatic smoke. They talked loudly and gaily and their cloaks dangled from their shoulders. The people made way for them. At the corner of Grafton Street a short fat man was putting two handsome ladies on a car in charge of another fat man. The car drove off and the short fat man caught sight of the party.

'André.'

'It's Farley!'

A torrent of talk followed. Farley was an American. No one knew very well what the talk was about. Villona and Rivière were the noisiest, but all the men were excited. They got up on a car, squeezing themselves together amid much laughter. They drove by the crowd, blended now into soft colours, to a music of merry bells. They took the train at Westland Row and in a few

seconds, as it seemed to Jimmy, they were walking out of
Kingstown Station. The ticket-collector saluted Jimmy; he was
an old man:

'Fine night, sir!'

It was a serene night; the harbour lay like a darkened mirror
at their feet. They proceeded towards it with linked arms, singing *Cadet Roussel* in chorus, stamping their feet at every:

'*Ho! Ho! Hohé, vraiment!*'

They got into a rowboat at the slip and made out for the
American's yacht. There was to be supper, music, cards.
Villona said with conviction:

'It is delightful!'

There was a yacht piano in the cabin. Villona played a waltz
for Farley and Rivière, Farley acting as cavalier and Rivière as
lady. Then an impromptu square dance, the men devising
original figures. What merriment! Jimmy took his part with a
will; this was seeing life, at least. Then Farley got out of breath
and cried '*Stop!*' A man brought in a light supper, and the
young men sat down to it for form's sake. They drank, however:
it was Bohemian. They drank Ireland, England, France, Hun-
gary, the United States of America. Jimmy made a speech, a
long speech, Villona saying: 'Hear! hear!' whenever there was a
pause. There was a great clapping of hands when he sat down.
It must have been a good speech. Farley clapped him on the
back and laughed loudly. What jovial fellows! What good
company they were!

Cards! cards! The table was cleared. Villona returned quietly
to his piano and played voluntaries for them. The other men
played game after game, flinging themselves boldly into the
adventure. They drank the health of the Queen of Hearts and of
the Queen of Diamonds. Jimmy felt obscurely the lack of an
audience: the wit was flashing. Play ran very high and paper
began to pass. Jimmy did not know exactly who was winning,
but he knew that he was losing. But it was his own fault, for he
frequently mistook his cards and the other men had to calculate
his IOUs for him. They were devils of fellows, but he wished
they would stop: it was getting late. Someone gave the toast of
the yacht *The Belle of Newport*, and then someone proposed one
great game for a finish.

The piano had stopped; Villona must have gone up on deck.
It was a terrible game. They stopped just before the end of it to
drink for luck. Jimmy understood that the game lay between

Routh and Ségouin. What excitement! Jimmy was excited too; he would lose, of course. How much had he written away? The men rose to their feet to play the last tricks, talking and gesticulating. Routh won. The cabin shook with the young men's cheering and the cards were bundled together. They began then to gather in what they had won. Farley and Jimmy were the heaviest losers.

He knew that he would regret in the morning, but at present he was glad of the rest, glad of the dark stupor that would cover up his folly. He leaned his elbows on the table and rested his head between his hands, counting the beats of his temples. The cabin door opened and he saw the Hungarian standing in a shaft of grey light:

'Daybreak, gentlemen!'

12
Ecce Puer[1]

ECCE PUER

Of the dark past
A child is born;
With joy and grief
My heart is torn.

Calm in his cradle
The living lies.
May love and mercy
Unclose his eyes!

Young life is breathed
On the glass;
The world that was not
Comes to pass.

A child is sleeping:
An old man gone.
O, father forsaken,
Forgive your son!

---

[1] 'Ecce puer' is Latin for 'Behold the boy'

13

Counterparts

The bell rang furiously and, when Miss Parker went to the
tube,[1] a furious voice called out in a piercing North of Ireland
accent:

'Send Farrington here!'

Miss Parker returned to her machine, saying to a man who
was writing at a desk:

'Mr Alleyne wants you upstairs.'

The man muttered '*Blast* him!' under his breath and pushed
back his chair to stand up. When he stood up he was tall and of
great bulk. He had a hanging face, dark wine-coloured, with
fair eyebrows and moustache: his eyes bulged forwards slightly
and the whites of them were dirty. He lifted up the counter and,
passing by the clients, went out of the office with a heavy step.

He went heavily upstairs until he came to the second landing,
where a door bore a brass plate with the inscription *Mr Alleyne*.
Here he halted, puffing with labour and vexation, and knocked.
The shrill voice cried:

'Come in!'

The man entered Mr Alleyne's room. Simultaneously Mr
Alleyne, a little man wearing gold-rimmed glasses on a clean-
shaven face, shot his head up over a pile of documents. The head
was so pink and hairless it seemed like a large egg reposing on
the papers. Mr Alleyne did not lose a moment:

'Farrington? What is the meaning of this? Why have I always
to complain of you? May I ask you why you haven't made a
copy of that contract between Bodley and Kirway? I told you
it must be ready by four o'clock.'

'But Mr Shelley said, sir . . .'

'*Mr Shelley said, sir* . . . Kindly attend to what I say and not to
what *Mr Shelley says*, sir. You have always some excuse or another for shirking work. Let me tell you that if the contract is
not copied before this evening I'll lay the matter before Mr
Crosbie . . . Do you hear me now?'

---

[1] a speaking-tube set up to communicate between different rooms

'Yes, sir.'

'Do you hear me now? . . . Ay and another little matter! I might as well be talking to the wall as talking to you. Understand once for all that you get a half an hour for your lunch and not an hour and a half. How many courses do you want, I'd like to know . . . Do you mind me now?'

'Yes, sir.'

Mr Alleyne bent his head again upon his pile of papers. The man stared fixedly at the polished skull which directed the affairs of Crosbie & Alleyne, gauging its fragility. A spasm of rage gripped his throat for a few moments and then passed, leaving after it a sharp sensation of thirst. The man recognized the sensation and felt that he must have a good night's drinking. The middle of the month was passed and, if he could get the copy done in time, Mr Alleyne might give him an order on the cashier. He stood still, gazing fixedly at the head upon the pile of papers. Suddenly Mr Alleyne began to upset all the papers, searching for something. Then, as if he had been unaware of the man's presence till that moment, he shot up his head again, saying:

'Eh? Are you going to stand there all day? Upon my word, Farrington, you take things easy!'

'I was waiting to see . . .'

'Very good, you needn't wait to see. Go downstairs and do your work.'

The man walked heavily towards the door and, as he went out of the room, he heard Mr Alleyne cry after him that if the contract was not copied by evening Mr Crosbie would hear of the matter.

He returned to his desk in the lower office and counted the sheets which remained to be copied. He took up his pen and dipped it in the ink, but he continued to stare stupidly at the last words he had written: *In no case shall the said Bernard Bodley be* . . . The evening was falling and in a few minutes they would be lighting the gas: then he could write. He felt that he must slake the thirst in his throat. He stood up from his desk and, lifting the counter as before, passed out of the office. As he was passing out the chief clerk looked at him inquiringly.

'It's all right, Mr Shelley,' said the man, pointing with his finger to indicate the objective of his journey.

The chief clerk glanced at the hat-rack, but, seeing the row complete, offered no remark. As soon as he was on the landing the man pulled a shepherd's plaid cap out of his pocket, put it on his head and ran quickly down the rickety stairs. From the street door he walked on furtively on the inner side of the path towards the corner and all at once dived into a doorway. He was now safe in the dark snug of O'Neill's shop, and, filling up the little window that looked into the bar with his inflamed face, the colour of dark wine or dark meat, he called out:

'Here, Pat, give us a g.p., like a good fellow.'

The curate[1] brought him a glass of plain porter.[2] The man drank it at a gulp and asked for a caraway seed. He put his penny on the counter and, leaving the curate to grope for it in the gloom, retreated out of the snug as furtively as he had entered it.

Darkness, accompanied by a thick fog, was gaining upon the dusk of February and the lamps in Eustace Street had been lit. The man went up by the houses until he reached the door of the office, wondering whether he could finish his copy in time. On the stairs a moist pungent odour of perfumes saluted his nose: evidently Miss Delacour had come while he was out in O'Neill's. He crammed his cap back again into his pocket and re-entered the office, assuming an air of absent-mindedness.

'Mr Alleyne has been calling for you,' said the chief clerk severely. 'Where were you?'

The man glanced at the two clients who were standing at the counter as if to intimate that their presence prevented him from answering. As the clients were both male the chief clerk allowed himself a laugh.

'I know that game,' he said. 'Five times in one day is a little bit . . . Well, you better look sharp and get a copy of our correspondence in the Delacour case for Mr Alleyne.'

This address in the presence of the public, his run upstairs and the porter he had gulped down so hastily confused the man and, as he sat down at his desk to get what was required, he realized how hopeless was the task of finishing his copy of the contract before half-past five. The dark damp night was coming and he longed to spend it in the bars, drinking with his friends amid the glare of gas and the clatter of glasses. He got out the Delacour correspondence and passed out of the office. He hoped Mr

[1] barman

[2] dark-brown malt liquor, similar to stout

Alleyne would not discover that the last two letters were missing.

The moist pungent perfume lay all the way up to Mr Alleyne's room. Miss Delacour was a middle-aged woman of Jewish appearance. Mr Alleyne was said to be sweet on her or on her money. She came to the office often and stayed a long time when she came. She was sitting beside his desk now in an aroma of perfumes, smoothing the handle of her umbrella and nodding the great black feather in her hat. Mr Alleyne had swivelled his chair round to face her and thrown his right foot jauntily upon his left knee. The man put the correspondence on the desk and bowed respectfully, but neither Mr Alleyne nor Miss Delacour took any notice of his bow. Mr Alleyne tapped a finger on the correspondence and then flicked it towards him as if to say: *That's all right, you can go.*

The man returned to the lower office and sat down again at his desk. He stared intently at the incomplete phrase: *In no case shall the said Bernard Bodley be* . . . and thought how strange it was that the last three words began with the same letter. The chief clerk began to hurry Miss Parker, saying she would never have the letter typed in time for post. The man listened to the clicking of the machine for a few minutes and then set to work to finish his copy. But his head was not clear and his mind wandered away to the glare and rattle of the public-house. It was a night for hot punches. He struggled on with his copy, but when the clock struck five he had still fourteen pages to write. Blast it! He couldn't finish it in time. He longed to execrate aloud, to bring his fist down on something violently. He was so enraged that he wrote *Bernard Bernard* instead of *Bernard Bodley* and had to begin again on a clean sheet.

He felt strong enough to clear out the whole office single-handed. His body ached to do something, to rush out and revel in violence. All the indignities of his life enraged him . . . Could he ask the cashier privately for an advance? No, the cashier was no good, no damn good: he wouldn't give an advance . . . He knew where he would meet the boys: Leonard and O'Halloran and Nosey Flynn. The barometer of his emotional nature was set for a spell of riot.

His imagination had so abstracted him that his name was called twice before he answered. Mr Alleyne and Miss Delacour were standing outside the counter and all the clerks had turned round in anticipation of something. The man got up from his desk. Mr Alleyne began a tirade of abuse, saying that two letters were missing. The man answered that he knew nothing about them, that he had made a faithful copy. The tirade continued: it was so bitter and violent that the man could hardly restrain his fist from descending upon the head of the manikin before him:

'I know nothing about any other two letters,' he said stupidly.

'*You – know – nothing*. Of course you know nothing,' said Mr Alleyne. 'Tell me,' he added, glancing first for approval to the lady beside him, 'do you take me for a fool? Do you think me an utter fool?'

The man glanced from the lady's face to the little egg-shaped head and back again; and, almost before he was aware of it, his tongue had found a felicitous moment:

'I don't think, sir,' he said, 'that that's a fair question to put to me.'

There was a pause in the very breathing of the clerks. Everyone was astounded (the author of the witticism no less than his neighbours) and Miss Delacour, who was a stout amiable person, began to smile broadly. Mr Alleyne flushed to the hue of a wild rose and his mouth twitched with a dwarf's passion. He shook his fist in the man's face till it seemed to vibrate like the knob of some electric machine:

'You impertinent ruffian! You impertinent ruffian! I'll make short work of you! Wait till you see! You'll apologize to me for your impertinence or you'll quit the office instanter.[1] You'll quit this, I'm telling you, or you'll apologize to me!'

He stood in a doorway opposite the office, watching to see if the cashier would come out alone. All the clerks passed out and finally the cashier came out with the chief clerk. It was no use trying to say a word to him when he was with the chief clerk. The man felt that his position was bad enough. He had been obliged to offer an abject apology to Mr Alleyne for his impertinence, but he knew what a hornets' nest the office would be for him. He could remember the way in which Mr Alleyne had hounded little Peake out of the office in order to make room for his own nephew. He felt savage and thirsty and revengeful, annoyed with himself and with everyone else. Mr Alleyne would never give him an hour's rest; his life would be a hell to him. He had made a proper fool of himself this time. Could he not keep his tongue in his cheek? But they had never pulled together

[1] Latin for 'immediately'

from the first, he and Mr Alleyne, ever since the day Mr Alleyne had overheard him mimicking his North of Ireland accent to amuse Higgins and Miss Parker; that had been the beginning of it. He might have tried Higgins for the money, but sure Higgins never had anything for himself. A man with two establishments to keep up, of course he couldn't. . . .

He felt his great body again aching for the comfort of the public-house. The fog had begun to chill him and he wondered could he touch Pat in O'Neill's. He could not touch him for more than a bob – and a bob was no use. Yet he must get money somewhere or other: he had spent his last penny for the g.p. and soon it would be too late for getting money anywhere. Suddenly, as he was fingering his watch chain, he thought of Terry Kelly's pawn-office in Fleet Street. That was the dart! Why didn't he think of it sooner?

He went through the narrow alley of Temple Bar quickly, muttering to himself that they could all go to hell because he was going to have a good night of it. The clerk in Terry Kelly's said *A crown!*[1] but the consignor[2] held out for six shillings; and in the end the six shillings was allowed him literally. He came out of the pawn-office joyfully, making a little cylinder of the coins between his thumb and fingers. In Westmoreland Street the footpaths were crowded with young men and women returning from business, and ragged urchins ran here and there yelling out the names of the evening editions. The man passed through the crowd, looking on the spectacle generally with proud satisfaction and staring masterfully at the office-girls. His head was full of the noises of tram-gongs and swishing trolleys and his nose already sniffed the curling fumes of punch. As he walked on he preconsidered the terms in which he would narrate the incident to the boys:

'So, I just looked at him – coolly, you know, and looked at her. Then I looked back at him again – taking my time, you know. "I don't think that that's a fair question to put to me," says I.'

Nosey Flynn was sitting up in his usual corner of Davy Byrne's, and, when he heard the story, he stood Farrington a half-one,[3] saying it was as smart a thing as ever he heard. Farrington stood a drink in his turn. After a while O'Halloran

---

[1] five old shillings (twenty-five new pence)

[2] person leaving the item in pawn

[3] a half pint

and Paddy Leonard came in and the story was repeated to them. O'Halloran stood tailors of malt, hot, all round and told the story of the retort he had made to the chief clerk when he was in Callan's of Fownes's Street; but, as the retort was after the manner of the liberal shepherds in the eclogues, he had to admit that it was not as clever as Farrington's retort. At this Farrington told the boys to polish off that and have another.

Just as they were naming their poisons who should come in but Higgins! Of course he had to join in with the others. The men asked him to give his version of it, and he did so with great vivacity for the sight of five small hot whiskies was very exhilarating. Everyone roared laughing when he showed the way in which Mr Alleyne shook his fist in Farrington's face. Then he imitated Farrington, saying, '*And here was my nabs,*[1] *as cool as you please,*' while Farrington looked at the company out of his heavy dirty eyes, smiling and at times drawing forth stray drops of liquor from his moustache with the aid of his lower lip.

When that round was over there was a pause. O'Halloran had money, but neither of the other two seemed to have any; so the whole party left the shop somewhat regretfully. At the corner of Duke Street Higgins and Nosey Flynn bevelled off to the left, while the other three turned back towards the city. Rain was drizzling down on the cold streets and, when they reached the Ballast Office, Farrington suggested the Scotch House. The bar was full of men and loud with the noise of tongues and glasses. The three men pushed past the whining match-sellers at the door and formed a little party at the corner of the counter. They began to exchange stories. Leonard introduced them to a young fellow named Weathers who was performing at the Tivoli as an acrobat and knockabout *artiste*. Farrington stood a drink all round. Weathers said he would take a small Irish and Apollinaris.[2] Farrington, who had definite notions of what was what, asked the boys would they have an Apollinaris too; but the boys told him to make theirs hot.[3] The talk became theatrical. O'Halloran stood a round and then Farrington stood another round, Weathers protesting that the hospitality was too Irish. He promised to get them in behind the scenes and introduce them to some nice girls. O'Halloran said that he and Leonard

[1] this fellow

[2] Irish whiskey mixed with a special mineral water called Apollinaris

[3] whiskey served with a little hot water

would go, but that Farrington wouldn't go because he was a married man; and Farrington's heavy dirty eyes leered at the company in token that he understood he was being chaffed. Weathers made them all have just one little tincture[1] at his expense and promised to meet them later on at Mulligan's in Poolbeg Street.

When the Scotch House closed they went round to Mulligan's. They went into the parlour at the back and O'Halloran ordered small hot specials all round. They were all beginning to feel mellow. Farrington was just standing another round when Weathers came back. Much to Farrington's relief he drank a glass of bitter this time. Funds were getting low, but they had enough to keep them going. Presently two young women with big hats and a young man in a check suit came in and sat at a table close by. Weathers saluted them and told the company that they were out of the Tivoli. Farrington's eyes wandered at every moment in the direction of one of the young women. There was something striking in her appearance. An immense scarf of peacock-blue muslin was wound round her hat and knotted in a great bow under her chin; and she wore bright yellow gloves, reaching to the elbow. Farrington gazed admiringly at the plump arm which she moved very often and with much grace; and when, after a little time, she answered his gaze he admired still more her large dark brown eyes. The oblique staring expression in them fascinated him. She glanced at him once or twice and, when the party was leaving the room, she brushed against his chair and said '*O, pardon!*' in a London accent. He watched her leave the room in the hope that she would look back at him, but he was disappointed. He cursed his want of money and cursed all the rounds he had stood, particularly all the whiskies and Apollinaris which he had stood to Weathers. If there was one thing that he hated it was a sponge. He was so angry that he lost count of the conversation of his friends.

When Paddy Leonard called him he found that they were talking about feats of strength. Weathers was showing his biceps muscle to the company and boasting so much that the other two had called on Farrington to uphold the national honour. Farrington pulled up his sleeve accordingly and showed his biceps muscle to the company. The two arms were examined and compared and finally it was agreed to have a trial of

[1] drink

strength. The table was cleared and the two men rested their elbows on it, clasping hands. When Paddy Leonard said '*Go!*' each was to try to bring down the other's hand on to the table. Farrington looked very serious and determined.

The trial began. After about thirty seconds Weathers brought his opponent's hand slowly down on to the table. Farrington's dark wine-coloured face flushed darker still with anger and humiliation at having been defeated by such a stripling.

'You're not to put the weight of your body behind it. Play fair,' he said.

'Who's not playing fair?' said the other.

'Come on again. The two best out of three.'

The trial began again. The veins stood out on Farrington's forehead, and the pallor of Weathers' complexion changed to peony. Their hands and arms trembled under the stress. After a long struggle. Weathers again brought his opponent's hand slowly on to the table. There was a murmur of applause from the spectators. The curate, who was standing beside the table, nodded his red head towards the victor and said with stupid familiarity:

'Ah! that's the knack!'

'What the hell do you know about it?' said Farrington fiercely, turning on the man. 'What do you put in your gab for?'

'Sh, sh!' said O'Halloran, observing the violent expression of Farrington's face. 'Pony up,[1] boys. We'll have just one little smahan[2] more and then we'll be off.'

A very sullen-faced man stood at the corner of O'Connell Bridge waiting for the little Sandymount tram to take him home. He was full of smouldering anger and revengefulness. He felt humiliated and discontented; he did not even feel drunk; and he had only twopence in his pocket. He cursed everything. He had done for himself in the office, pawned his watch, spent all his money; and he had not even got drunk. He began to feel thirsty again and he longed to be back again in the hot reeking public-house. He had lost his reputation as a strong man, having been defeated twice by a mere boy. His heart swelled with fury and, when he thought of the woman in the big hat

[1] settle the bill

[2] drink

who had brushed against him and said *Pardon!* his fury nearly choked him.

His tram let him down at Shelbourne Road and he steered his great body along in the shadow of the wall of the barracks. He loathed returning to his home. When he went in by the side-door he found the kitchen empty and the kitchen fire nearly out. He bawled upstairs:

'Ada! Ada!'

His wife was a little sharp-faced woman who bullied her husband when he was sober and was bullied by him when he was drunk. They had five children. A little boy came running down the stairs.

'Who is that?' said the man, peering through the darkness.

'Me, pa.'

'Who are you? Charlie?'

'No, pa. Tom.'

'Where's your mother?'

'She's out at the chapel.'

'That's right . . . Did she think of leaving any dinner for me?'

'Yes, pa. I – '

'Light the lamp. What do you mean by having the place in darkness? Are the other children in bed?'

The man sat down heavily on one of the chairs while the little boy lit the lamp. He began to mimic his son's flat accent, saying half to himself: '*At the chapel. At the chapel, if you please!*' When the lamp was lit he banged his fist on the table and shouted:

'What's for my dinner?'

'I'm going . . . to cook it, pa,' said the little boy.

The man jumped up furiously and pointed to the fire.

'On that fire! You let the fire out! By God, I'll teach you to do that again!'

He took a step to the door and seized the walking-stick which was standing behind it.

'I'll teach you to let the fire out!' he said, rolling up his sleeve in order to give his arm free play.

The little boy cried '*O, pa!*' and ran whimpering round the table, but the man followed him and caught him by the coat. The little boy looked about him wildly but, seeing no way of escape, fell upon his knees.

'Now, you'll let the fire out the next time!' said the man, striking at him vigorously with the stick. 'Take that, you little whelp!'

The boy uttered a squeal of pain as the stick cut his thigh. He clasped his hands together in the air and his voice shook with fright.

'O, pa!' he cried. 'Don't beat me, pa! And I'll . . . I'll say a *Hail Mary*[1] for you . . . I'll say a *Hail Mary* for you, pa, if you don't beat me . . . I'll say a *Hail Mary*. . . .'

---

[1] a prayer to the Virgin Mary, repeated as a penance

Joyce's Dublin

These photographs show Dublin at the turn of the century when Joyce was growing up in the town.

CUSTOM HOUSE. DUBLIN. 4826. W.L.

KE IN S.T STEPHEN'S GREEN PARK DUBLIN.   L.S.

The Photographs

More About the Writing

1 The Sisters

James Joyce had two great-aunts whose maiden names had been Flynn. As Mrs Callanan and Mrs Lyons they ran a small music school in Dublin. In some remote corner of their family there had also been a priest who had suffered terrible doubts about the effectiveness of his ministry. Such were the broad hints from which Joyce constructed this story.

page 6 Rosicrucian: the Rosicrucians were originally a semi-religious society whose members claimed to have secret and magical knowledge. Perhaps his uncle uses the word to allude to what he regards as the unhealthily secretive discussions the boy was accustomed to having with Father Flynn on religious matters.

page 7 'It began to confess to me': a curious reversal of roles, since the boy would normally have confessed his sins to the priest in order to gain forgiveness and to clear his conscience of anything he had done wrong.

page 12 'It was that chalice he broke': Father Flynn apparently dropped the communion chalice while celebrating Mass – a very unfortunate accident – though some people said that the boy assisting him in the service was in fact to blame.

2 An Encounter

In June 1895 James and his younger brother Stanislaus decided to play truant from Belvedere College, and to walk to the Pigeon House, a power station situated on the outskirts of Dublin near the mouth of the River Liffey. It was while they were on this jaunt that James, who was thirteen years old, and Stanislaus, who was eleven, became involved in the events described in this story. Joyce wrote 'An Encounter' about ten years later, digging carefully into his memory for details of the places and events and especially of the people involved. Joe and Leo Dillon, for example, were based on boys from the neighbourhood in which the Joyce family was living at the time.

3 The Pandying

From 1888 until 1891, when he was nine, Joyce was a boarder at
Clongowes Wood College, the leading Catholic preparatory
school in Ireland. The school was run by Jesuits (priests and lay
members of the Society of Jesus, a religious order founded in
1534 by St Ignatius Loyola), and the boys were given a strict
and vigorous religious upbringing. James was not happy there
at first; he had not been there long before the incidents described in this extract from *A Portrait of the Artist as a Young Man*
took place. As time passed, however, he adjusted rather better
to his life away from home, and he became a very promising
pupil. As with 'An Encounter', Joyce's memory of the places and
people involved seems to have been exact. The prefect of studies
(Father Dolan in the story) was in real life Father James Daly,
and the rector (or principal) of the college was the Reverend
John Conmee. As in all the extracts from *Portrait of the Artist*,
James is represented by the figure of Stephen Dedalus.

page 21 'Was that sin . . . different kinds of hats': young Stephen
has been taught that anger is a sin and that people must confess to a priest if they wish to be forgiven for an angry word or
deed. To carry out this confession, they have to go to church at
a particular time to see the priest. What if the priest himself is
guilty of anger, however? This is the question that enters
Stephen's mind at this point in the story. Perhaps Father
Arnall's anger isn't a sin because he only employs it to try to
make the boys work harder. But suppose he should be angry
sometime without a good reason? Then, the boy imagines, he
would have to go and confess to a minister, a priest of higher
rank than himself. He considers the further possibility of a
minister needing to confess to *his* superior, the rector – and so
on, right up to the head of the Society of Jesus, the general of the
order.

page 25 'got the card . . . Yorkists': Stephen is doubly hurt – not
only because he has been pandied, but also because he has up to
now been regarded as a hard worker, always coming near the
top of the class, and is a leader among the other boys of his
group.

page 26 'The senate and Roman people declared': decisions in
ancient Rome were always made in the name of the senate (a
sort of parliament composed of members of the most noble
families) and people. The boy from the 'second of grammar'
uses this expression to show that everyone agreed that Stephen

had been badly treated. He is voicing their collective opinion
page 29 Hamilton Rowan was an eighteenth-century Irish
patriot who had sheltered at the castle while being pursued and
fired on by British soldiers.
'ghost in the white cloak of a marshal': one member of the
family that had owned Clongowes Castle long before it became
a school had been a marshal in the Austrian army. His ghost
was said to haunt the house.

4 Araby
The Joyce family lived in North Richmond Street, Dublin,
from 1894 until 1898. It was while they were there that James
and Stanislaus had played truant from Belvedere College
and encountered the 'queer old josser' down by the river bank.
The events described in 'Araby' might similarly be based on
James's own experiences – but, unfortunately, there is no proof
as to whether they are or not. They might have happened to
any boy in his early teens who had fallen in love for the first
time. Certainly a fête called 'Araby in Dublin' took place in
1894; its aim was to raise funds for a local hospital.
page 37 'some Freemason affair': Freemasons were (and are)
disapproved of in many religious circles. They are members of a
semi-secret brotherhood devoted to mutual aid.

5 Visits
This extract from *A Portrait of the Artist as a Young Man* takes the
form of a succession of imagined flashbacks in Stephen's mind
to occasions in his early adolescence. Although he is becoming
aware of girls, he has as yet no girlfriend of his own. He has been
much impressed by reading Alexandre Dumas's *The Count of
Monte Cristo* and has become infatuated with the character of
Mercedes, the heroine of that novel. He has even wandered
about the locality where he lives half-heartedly looking for her,
as a substitute for plucking up the courage to talk to a real girl.
Together with the usual sexual fantasies experienced by
adolescent boys, these thoughts about Mercedes preoccupy
Stephen. They worry him, too, and he becomes inwardly guilty
at the secretive nature of his imaginings.

7 The Night of The Whitsuntide Play
During the years that Joyce attended Belvedere College, the

rector there was a certain Father Henry. Although the young James had a very different attitude to him from that which he displayed towards Father Daly at Clongowes, he seems to have been hauled before the rector for disciplinary reasons on more than one occasion. Far from instilling in him a profound respect for Father Henry, however, these brushes with authority tended to encourage James to bait the master all the more. This situation came to a head when, towards the end of his time at Belvedere, James took part in a school production of F. Anstey's play *Vice-Versa*. In it, he took the part of a schoolmaster and, prompted by his friends the brothers Albrecht and Vincent Connolly, he decided to take off Father Henry, mimicking his gestures and the sound of his voice from the stage.

page 54 'The Blessed Sacrament . . . tabernacle': the tabernacle is a small cupboard on the altar in which the bread and wine (the sacrament) is kept for communion. At Belvedere College, the chapel and vestry were used as changing rooms when plays were being put on, and the performers gathered there before going on to the stage. On such occasions the bread and wine were removed from the tabernacle in case anyone who was not a priest should feel inclined to interfere with them.

page 56 'the incommunicable emotion which had been the cause of his day's unrest': as in both the extract entitled 'Visits' and also the events which follow in this particular episode, Stephen's restless feelings seem to be centred on his thoughts about girls in general and one special girl in particular. This is perhaps why he is so impatient at the idea of a small boy dressing as a girl to perform a dance during the first part of the evening's entertainment.

page 58 'their leavetaking on the steps of the tram at Harold's Cross': the incident which forms the last episode of the section entitled 'Visits'.

* * * * * Heron's words and action at this point cause Stephen's thoughts to flash back to an earlier occasion in his life when he had been tormented and beaten in an effort – unsuccessful as it happens – to make him admit that the poet Byron was 'no good'. After some moments, omitted from this extract, he turns back to the present.

8 A Mother

page 66 Irish Revival: the time during the late nineteenth and early twentieth centuries when the movement for an Ireland independent of the British crown was becoming increasingly popular, and along with it an interest in native Irish art forms.

9 Poems from Pomes Penyeach

Nora Barnacle bore Joyce a son (Giorgio) and a daughter (Lucia). The two poems printed in this section reflect the tenderness and affection Joyce felt for his children. Both were written while the family was living in Italy. *A Flower given to my Daughter* recalls with touching simplicity a moment, while Joyce was teaching in Trieste, when one of his pupils, Amalia Popper, gave Lucia a rose. It was a beautiful gesture; as Joyce wrote in his notebook 'Frail gift, frail giver, frail blue-veined child'. Indeed, Lucia suffered from a variety of mental disorders throughout her life, causing Joyce considerable concern.

The fact that Giorgio was altogether more robust, however, did not prevent Joyce's feelings of fatherly protectiveness from welling up from time to time, as they do in *On the Beach at Fontana*.

10 A Trip To Cork

The events described in this extract actually took place when James was twelve years old. As the family fortunes declined, his father (pictured here as Simon Dedalus) was obliged to auction his few remaining properties in his home town of Cork. So, in February 1894, father and son set off to see to the business. While they were in Cork, John Joyce, full of rather forced high spirits, took the opportunity of introducing his son to some of his old haunts and to not a few of his old friends. But it was in no sense a happy time for the boy, who was still being pursued by some of the secretive and worrying feelings about sex and about girls that he had entertained earlier (as recounted in 'Visits' and 'The Night of the Whitsuntide Play').

11 After The Race

The background to 'After the Race' is real enough even though the principal events themselves are fictitious. The race for the Gordon Bennett International Automobile Racing Cup was held on 2 July 1903, and the results were exactly as Joyce records them here: 1st, Germany; 2nd, 3rd, 4th, France; 5th, Great Britain.

12 Ecce Puer

Two days before the end of 1931, John Joyce, James's father
died. Just over six weeks later, Stephen James Joyce, the
writer's grandson, was born. In commemoration and celebration
of the two events, Joyce wrote this wonderfully simple account
of his thoughts and feelings and emotions.

13 Counterparts

The precise events of 'Counterparts' are probably fictitious
though the figure of Farrington is based on Joyce's uncle
William Murray. It was this man's son who is supposed in real
life to have cried out 'I'll say a *Hail Mary* for you, pa, if you
don't beat me'. As elsewhere, Joyce builds up his story from a
few hints and ideas gleaned from his own knowledge and
experience.

Thoughts and Developments and Suggestions for Writing*

Finding Out

1 The Sisters

(a) '*It had always sounded strangely in my ears*' (page 5)

The small boy in this story is worried by the idea of paralysis. Not only is the word itself strange to his ears, but the very notion of the condition of paralysis of which he has no experience troubles him.

Are you worried in a similar way by the thought of disease or deformity, of a particular disease or a particular deformity? Can you recall a time when you have been fascinated by the idea of something which we normally reckon to be very unpleasant, like an illness of some sort? Have you ever been frightened by someone who was deformed?

(b) '*Tiresome old fool!*' (page 5)

When you were younger (or perhaps even more recently) was there some older person – a friend of your parents perhaps, or a relative – whom you liked at first, but who became a nuisance by always talking about the same subject? What do you dislike most about older people? Do you think it natural that young people should be impatient with the ideas and attitudes of their elders? Can you foresee that you might one day become boring or annoying to those who are younger than you? Do you have a pet subject which you enjoy talking about, but which others, even those of your own age, find boring?

(c) '*The youngster and he were great friends*' (page 6)

Have you ever had an adult friend in whom you could confide and whom you regarded as very important and close to you? Do you have one now? What is it that attracts you to him or her? What do other people think about your friendship?

Who (other than your parents or relatives) has had the

most influence on you in the course of your life so far
among the adults you have known?

(d) '*I drew the blankets over my head and tried to think of Christmas*'
(pages 6–7)

Do you remember an occasion when you have been plagued
with unpleasant thoughts at night time? What brought
them about? What did you do to dispel them? Have you
ever had a particularly unpleasant nightmare? Have you a
dream that recurs night after night? What is the pleasantest
thing that you try to conjure up when you are having a bad
night?

(e) '*I went in on tiptoe*' (page 9)

Have you ever visited a house where there has recently been
a death? What was it like? What were your reactions when
you got there?

Have you ever visited someone – perhaps an elderly member
of your own family – who was seriously ill? What were your
reactions? Recall a time when you have visited a very sick
person in hospital. What is your attitude to hospitals in
general?

(f) '*He had his mind set on that*' (page 11)

Have you ever known someone to have set their mind on
achieving something which everyone else knew to be
impossible? Have you ever set your mind on something in
this way? Should we encourage people to think they can
achieve things which everyone else knows they cannot and
never will achieve?

Small children – even older ones and adults too – sometimes get it into their heads that they want to do something
which is quite out of the question. Teenagers get wild ideas
about what they intend to do later in life. How should they
be treated? Should we always be practical and destroy one
another's illusions? Or should we allow other people to have
their dreams?

Do you have an ambition, a dream or a desire which, when
you think about it, you admit is impossible? How do your
friends regard it? How do your parents and other adults
regard it? If it is impossible, what makes you cling to it?

(g) *Suggestions for writing:*
Accident
'Tiresome old fool!'
Fever

Nightmares
Casualty Ward
The Impossible Dream
I want to be . . .
An Unusual Friend
The Dwarf
A Death in the Family
Grandfather

2 An Encounter

(a) '*Everyone was incredulous when it was reported that he had a vocation for the priesthood*' (page 13)

Have you ever been surprised at the jobs your friends or relations have taken up after leaving school? Why?

Are you ever surprised to find that certain of your friends excel at particular subjects at school?

What leads people to associate certain types of people with certain types of work? What is it that makes us consider that particular individuals *look* as if they do particular jobs – bank clerks or insurance agents and so on? Why is it important that people of a certain temperament should undertake certain types of work? What, for instance, in your opinion, ought a good priest to be like? What qualities does a good schoolteacher need? Do you think that the adults with whom you come most closely in contact are effective in the jobs they do? Have you ever asked them when and how it was that they started in that job?

(b) '*I planned a day's miching*' (page 14)

Have you ever deliberately played truant from school? Or do you know of someone who has done so, and later told you all the details? Were you or they found out?

Have you ever gone off to enjoy yourself, letting your parents think that you were doing something else? What were the thoughts in the back of your mind that made you want to break out?

Have you ever thought about running away from home to do something much more exciting with your life than you do at present? Have you ever actually left home, even for a short while, intending never to return? What were your parents' reactions?

(c) '*I saw a man approaching from the far end of the field*' (page 17)

Have you ever had an encounter of the sort the boys have in

this story? Have you ever met someone (either like this or in more ordinary circumstances) whom you have found quite pleasant at first, but of whom you have become quite frightened because of his or her behaviour as time went on? What is your attitude to people when you meet them for the first time? Do you like to find out as much about them as possible – their way of life, their interests, their opinions – or are you inclined to be shy of entering into discussion with them?

What qualities in people make them most attractive to you? Do you think people always give the impression of being better or more pleasant than they really are to create an effect for the benefit of others? Do you ever put on an act in this way to impress other people?

(d) *'let you be Murphy and I'll be Smith'* (page 19)

Have you ever given a false name when you got into trouble of some sort? Did it help, or were you found out in the end? What is the worst trouble you have ever been in? What happened?

How do people normally react when they are put on the spot or caught red-handed? How do your friends or class-mates react when a teacher catches them out? What is the best way to behave when you get into trouble, whether you deserve it or not?

Are people in authority, like the police or parents or teachers, always fair in the way they deal with you under these circumstances? What would you do if you were in a position of authority and you had to deal with someone who had done something wrong?

(e) *'Now my heart beat as he came running across the field to me!'* (page 20)

Have you ever been glad of the company of one of your friends at some particularly tricky moment? Why is it better to have other people around when things begin to be difficult? The narrator in this story says that he was glad of Mahony's support even though he did not particularly like him sometimes. Can you recall an occasion when your relationship with someone improved as a result of some problem you shared? Does enduring difficulties together make for better friendships between people than might arise in the ordinary run of events?

(f) *Suggestions for writing*:
Breaking out!
An Unpleasant Encounter
A New Friend
Caught in the Act!
Accidental Meeting
Getting to know you . . .
The Stranger
My Best Friend
The Ordeal

3 The Pandying

(a) '*He could not speak with fright*' (page 23)

Have you ever been so frightened that you could not speak?
Was your fear justified or did you afterwards have a good
laugh about it?

What is the most frightening thing you can remember?
What were your reactions on that occasion?

Have you ever known anyone to be frightened unneces-
sarily – a younger brother or sister perhaps – whom you
were able to calm down? How did you do so? Have you
ever frightened someone else? Was it on purpose or by
accident?

(b) '*Out with your hand this moment!*' (page 24)

What is the most effective way you have ever been
punished? What were the circumstances? Why do you think
that particular punishment was most effective in your case?
Should the punishment always be made to fit the crime?

Are there any circumstances when you think people ought
not to be punished even though they have been guilty of
some offence and admit as much?

What punishments do you have given to you at home when
you do something wrong? Do your parents or older brothers
or sisters stay angry with you for long when they punish
you? Do your teachers? Or do they become calm and
friendly again as soon as the moment of punishment is
over? Which is better, do you think? If you become angry
with someone for a good reason, does your anger last for
long, or are you able to get it out of your system fairly
quickly and to return to a pleasant manner?

(c) '*I wouldn't stand it*' (page 26)

Can you recall an occasion when you were encouraged by

135

someone to do something about which you weren't quite certain?

Have you ever encouraged someone else to follow a particular course of action when they were hesitating over doing so? Were you right to do it?

Have you ever been persuaded to do something which was in fact wrong?

Have you ever encouraged someone to do something against his better judgement which went badly wrong? What did you do to help put things right?

(d) '*Come in!*' (page 29)

Can you recall an interview with someone of whom you were rather afraid? How did you feel as you approached the time and place of the encounter? How did you react during the meeting? Was your fear justified?

What were your reactions during your first day at a new school or in a job during the holidays? Was everyone sympathetic with you, or were there some people who went out of their way to make things difficult?

Have you ever complained about the unfairness of a schoolteacher to someone in higher authority? Have you ever complained about one of your family or friends to your parents or some other adult?

Do you think it is better to complain when you think something is unfair or wrong, or do you think it is better to grin and bear it?

(e) '*He broke into a run . . .*' (page 31)

Have you ever won a victory of the sort Stephen wins in this story? Do you think it is good to display your feelings when you have won a victory of some sort, or do you think it is better to remain quiet and let the moment pass?

How have you felt when some rival has won a victory over you? Did you think he or she was right or even fair to make a fuss about winning?

(f) '*They made a cradle of their locked hands*' (page 31)

Have you ever been a popular hero for some reason, even for a short while? Did you enjoy the moment or were you embarrassed?

Does success spoil people? Can you think of an occasion when someone you know (even yourself maybe) behaved badly because success went to his head?

Do you like the limelight? Do you aim to be a school prefect or a house captain or even school captain? What makes good prefects or captains? How do you think they should be selected? Do your friends and acquaintances always behave well and live up to what is expected of them when they reach positions of responsibility?

(g) *Suggestions for writing:*
Scared stiff!
The Joke that went Wrong
Unfair!
Friendly Persuasion
The Loser
Hero
Getting over it
'I wouldn't stand it'
The Interview
Family Feuds
Panic!
Grin and bear it!

Loves and Conflicts

4 Araby

(a) '*Every morning I lay on the floor in the front parlour watching her door*' (page 36)

Have you ever watched someone from a distance because you were too shy to approach and speak to them? What were the circumstances? Who was the person – an adult who seemed far too remote and forbidding for you to strike up a conversation, or perhaps a boy or girl whom you wanted to get to know but of whom you were rather shy? How did you get over the problem?

Have you ever tried to engineer a meeting with a boy or girl whom you wanted to get to know? What did you do?

(b) '*I thought little of the future*' (page 36)

What is your attitude to the future? Do you make careful plans or do you let things happen as they come?

Does having a boy- or girl-friend make any difference to your attitude to the future? Do you try to plan things more carefully so that you have more free time to spend with them?

Do your plans always work out properly? What is your

reaction when things go wrong after careful planning? Has this ever happened to you because of the thoughtlessness of your friend? What did you do?

Do you enjoy making plans together with your boy- or girl-friend? What sort of plans are they? Do they always work out?

(c) '*O love! O love!*' (page 37)

Do you consider that you have ever been in love? How can you tell that you are in love with someone? What sort of difference to you did being in love make? Was your being in love obvious to other people – friends, family?

Have you ever felt attracted to someone who did not return your feelings? How did you feel when they told you that they were just not interested in you? Did this make any difference to your attitude to starting up any other relationship?

(d) '*I sat staring at the clock for some time . . .*' (page 38)

Are you good at keeping appointments? Can you recall an occasion when you were late and ruined someone else's day or evening as a result?

Has your enjoyment ever been ruined because you were late for an appointment or a train or a meeting? What were your feelings when you discovered that you were too late? What did you do instead?

What is your attitude when your girl- or boy-friend is late for a date?

Are you a patient sort of person or not? Do you find it difficult to wait for the time for some important event to come round?

(e) '*my eyes burned with anguish and anger*' (page 40)

Have you ever been bitterly disappointed? How did you get over it?

What sort of things cause people the greatest disappointments?

Have your parents ever been badly disappointed? What were the circumstances? How did they react? Did it affect you in any way?

What effect does it have on you for someone to say that they are disappointed in you or in your work or in your behaviour?

(f) *Suggestions for writing:*
Making Plans

The First Meeting
Impatience
Disaster!
Boyfriend
Girlfriend
Being Let Down
Shy
Getting over a Disappointment

5 Visits

(a) '*The furniture had been hustled out*' (page 41)

What do you remember about some occasion when your family moved house? Did you enjoy the experience? Did it take you long to settle in to your new area?

In what ways can moving be a depressing occasion? Why do people usually move house? What do you dislike most about moving?

(b) '*some duty was being laid upon his shoulders*' (page 41)

Do your parents ever discuss their problems with you? How do you react? Do you merely listen or do you join in the discussions and suggest solutions? Are there matters which your parents are quite ready to discuss with you which they never discuss with your younger brothers or sisters?

Have your parents ever discussed family matters seriously with you in order to prepare you for changes which they want to bring about? What sort of things have been involved? Do your parents expect certain things of you – a certain degree of achievement, a certain standard of work, or behaviour, or support when they want to undertake something difficult? Do you think it right that parents should expect their children to do things for them? Will you expect your children to work hard or behave well to please you?

Are there any things at which you excel within your family circle? Are these things always left for you to do? Why is it that you are particularly good at them?

(c) '*Dublin was a new and complex sensation*' (page 41)

How do you go about exploring a new area? Are you good at remembering your way about places? Recount an occasion when you got seriously lost in a place which was new to you.

When you have nothing to do, do you sometimes wander off across country or around the streets of a town or city in order to kill time?

Are you ever bored at home? What do you do to dispel the boredom? What do you do to fill your time when you are on holiday from school but there is no one about to talk to or play with? How do you react when your parents or other adults try to occupy you or give you jobs to do?

(d) '*She told too of certain changes they had seen in her of late*' (page 43)

Have *you* changed? Have other people noticed a change in your manner or character in the course of time?

Have you noticed changes in other people in this way? Do you have a friend or relative whom you have known for some years who has changed as far as his or her attitude to you is concerned? Can you think of any explanation for this?

To what extent are the changes you think you see in others really due to changes taking place in you?

(e) '*he felt himself a gloomy figure*' (page 44)

Recount an occasion when you felt out of place in the way Stephen does at the children's party. Was it your fault or that of the people you were with?

Do you enjoy being something of an individualist, a loner, or do you prefer to be one in a crowd, and to identify with a group of friends?

What does it feel like to be left out of things on purpose by your fellows, because of something you have said or done to arouse their hostility? Can you think of an occasion when you have been deliberately left out of something very enjoyable because of your unpopularity among your friends? Or among the members of your family?

(f) '*It was the last tram*' (page 44)

In this story, James Joyce tells how Stephen reacted to a moment of intense pleasure at being with the girl he was beginning to fall in love with: he noticed the details of their being together precisely, and Joyce records the circumstances of the tram journey minutely. Can you recall an occasion when you were very happy in the company of someone else?

(g) '*But he did neither*' (page 45)

Was there a time that you can recall when you were unable to pluck up the courage to do something which would have given you a great deal of satisfaction?

How do people react when they miss important opportunities? Do you react in any special way? Do you show your feelings at all or do you tend to bottle them up?

(h) *Suggestions for writing:*

On the Move
Family Conference
The Outsider
Wandering
A Missed Opportunity
Unpopularity
A Happy Moment
Responsibilities
A Change for the Worse
A Different Person
A New Home
Lost!

6 Poems from 'Chamber Music'

(a) '*The old piano plays an air,*
     Sedate and slow and gay;
   She bends upon the yellow keys,
     Her head inclines this way.' (page 47)

Is there a special picture in your mind, a memory of a particular moment you have shared with someone, which has become identified completely with that person to the exclusion of everything and everyone else?

When you think of people whom you have not seen for some time, what pictures of experiences shared with them come to mind?

Do particular pieces of music remind you of particular people? Do certain objects in day-to-day life, or certain objects that you have collected over the years, remind you of people you have known?

(b) '*My book is closed;*
     I read no more' (page 48)

Have you ever given up doing something for good as a result of the influence of a girl- or boy-friend? Was it a good thing you did so?

Are you a good influence on your friends, or do you lead them into trouble?

What is the opinion of other people who know you both of your relationship with your girl- or boy-friend?

(c) '*Love is unhappy when love is away!*' (page 50)

How do you react to separation from someone you are fond of? Are you unbearable towards everyone else? Can you concentrate on your work? Does separation make all that much difference to you, or do you simply look forward to the next time you will meet and get on with life in the meantime?

(d) '*He is a stranger to me now*
    Who was my friend' (page 51)

Have you ever lost good friends as a result of taking up with a new girl- or boy-friend?

Have you ever parted company with your group of friends because someone you were fond of disapproved of them? Or have you done the opposite and parted with a girl- or boy-friend because they did not fit in with the rest of your circle of friends?

Have you ever parted company with a good friend because he or she was a rival for the affection of someone else?

(e) '*My love, my love, my love, why have you left me alone?*' (page 53)

What are your reactions on parting company with a boy- or girl-friend for good? If someone says he or she doesn't want to see you again, do you try to persuade them otherwise? Does this sort of reaction work? How would you behave towards other people or towards your work if this were to happen to you?

(f) *Suggestions for writing:*
    Snapshots
    Breaking Up
    Losing Friends
    Being Apart
    Souvenirs
    A Good Influence

7 The Night of the Whitsuntide Play

(a) '*He passed out of the schoolhouse and halted under the shed that flanked the garden*' (page 55)

Have you ever taken part in a play or a concert or some other activity where you were performing in front of a large audience? How did you feel as you waited for your turn to perform? How did you occupy your time?

Are you the sort of person who likes to perform on the stage in public? What attracts you to doing so? Do you belong to a drama group or orchestra or choir in your school? Do you belong to one out of school?

What is your attitude to the hours of rehearsal that are often involved?

(b) *'you can take him off rippingly'* (page 56)

Do you have a particular talent that makes you popular with your friends? What is it? Can you recall an occasion when you particularly enjoyed performing for their benefit? Or can you think of a time when doing so led to an embarrassing situation? Do you ever find that being asked to perform by your friends is a nuisance, and that you begin to regret having the talent at all?

(c) *'The rivals were school friends'* (page 57)

Do you have a particular friend at school who is also your chief rival, at work, perhaps, or at games? Does your friendship ever suffer as a result of your rivalry? Do other people, particularly teachers, know of your rivalry and encourage it? Do you think it is an advantage to have a friendly rival in this way? Do you tend to make friends with people who are as good as you are (or perhaps as bad!) at work or games? Or do you make friends irrespective of their interests and abilities?

Have you ever had a friend whom you lost because either you or he began to do much better in a sphere where you had formerly been close rivals?

(d) *'A shaft of momentary anger flew through Stephen's mind'* (page 58)

Can you recall an occasion when you became angry with a friend because he teased you in front of a stranger? Did you show your anger?

Do you have a friend whom you find particularly easy to tease? Why is that? Has he or she ever had a row with you because the teasing became unbearable?

Do your parents or brothers or sisters tease you? Do you ever get into trouble for teasing a younger brother or sister?

(e) *'the poem he had written about it'* (page 58)

Do you ever write poetry – not so much at school, but at home, in private, perhaps as an outlet for your feelings about someone? What makes you want to write poetry? What makes writing a poem about someone you are fond of important?

Do you ever show your private poetry to anyone else?

If you don't write poetry, is there something else perhaps which you do in private, such as writing music, or writing plays or stories, or drawing? Why do you keep it private? When do you chiefly feel you want to do it?

(f) '*That's no way to send for one of the senior boys*' (page 59)

Do you ever feel annoyed if you are spoken to or treated as if you were younger than you are? What sort of person tends to treat you in this way? Why do you suppose they do so?

Have you ever seen an older boy or girl at your school talked down to by one of the teachers? What was their reaction? Did you sympathise with them?

Do you find that older pupils tend to treat you in a similar way, by *telling* you to do things rather than *asking* you, for instance, or by omitting to say 'please' or 'thank you'? How do you react to their manner? Will you do the same as you grow older?

(g) '*A few moments after he found himself on the stage*' (page 61)

Have you ever taken part in a play or concert when someone special was in the audience? Did their presence make a difference to your performance?

How does it feel to be in the audience when someone you know well and are fond of is performing?

Have you ever been in the audience when your boy- or girl-friend made a disastrous mistake in a play or concert? How did you react? What did you say to him or her afterwards?

(h) '*I have to leave a message*' (page 61)

Can you recall an occasion when you made excuses to your parents or friends in order to conceal the fact that you were meeting your boy- or girl-friend? What did you tell them? Did they ever find out the truth?

Have you ever been seen by friends when you were out with your girl-friend or boy-friend after you had told them that you were going to do something completely different? How did they react when they saw you? How did they react later when they saw you alone?

(i) '*He hardly knew where he was walking*' (page 61)

Have you ever been so upset or annoyed that you walked off without realising where you were heading? Does walking help to calm you down when you have been upset?

For what other reasons do you go for walks alone?

(j) *Suggestions for writing*.
   The Night of the Play
   An Embarrassing Occasion
   Rivals
   The Tease
   Cooling Off
   The Play Group
   In the Audience
   Discovered!

Parents

8 A Mother

(a) '*She had tact*' (page 67)

How important is tact when dealing with people? Can you recall an occasion when you have needed to be very tactful? Or can you think of a time when either you or a friend were very tactless?

Do you need to employ tact just as much when dealing with people much younger than yourself as when you are dealing with those who are older than you?

Can you recall a time when someone treated you in a tactless fashion? What were your reactions? Were they aware that they had behaved tactlessly? What did they do to put things right, if anything?

(b) '*everything that was to be done was done*' (page 67)

How reliable are you? Do other people tend to look upon you as someone who will always see a task through efficiently? Or are you rather careless about such things and regarded as being unreliable in general? Do you think you deserve your reputation?

Do you know of some other person who is invaluable when it comes to organising things, someone of whom people can safely say 'Leave it to him (or her)'?

What is your opinion of such people? Do you tend to rely on them or do you prefer to do things for yourself?

(c) '*She was glad that he had suggested coming with her*' (page 69)

Are there ever occasions when you very much value the presence and moral support of someone else? What sort of occasions are these? What sort of person do you like to have with you – or doesn't it matter so long as there *is* someone else?

Are you the sort of person other people like to have around to support them? Why is this – because of your size and strength, or because you are good in an argument, or because you command respect? Do you enjoy being in this sort of position? Have you ever let anyone down when they were specially relying on you?

(d) '*He was extremely nervous*' (page 70)

Can you recall an occasion when you were very nervous for some reason? What were the circumstances? How did you get over your nervousness?

Do you find it easy to conceal nervousness?

Have you ever been made nervous simply because someone else you were with was in a nervous state? How do you react when one of your parents or some other older person becomes nervous?

(e) '*Mr Holohan said that it wasn't his business*' (page 71)

Have you ever been in a similar situation to Mrs Kearney, where someone tried to get out of an awkward situation you had placed them in by pretending it was no business of his or hers?

Have you ever pretended you were not responsible for something that other people were getting at you over, when in fact you *were* responsible all the time? Was your deception successful? How did you feel afterwards – did you have a conscience over the matter or did you feel pleased with yourself?

(f) '*he had to ask her to lower her voice*' (page 72)

Do you remember an occasion when you have been embarrassed by the fuss being made by someone you were with? Was the fuss being made on your behalf?

Have you ever caused embarrassment to someone else by causing trouble of some sort while they were present?

(g) '*Kathleen looked down moving the point of her new shoe*' (page 73)

Have you ever been put into an embarrassing situation by the public behaviour of one of your parents? Were they justified in behaving the way they did? Did you try to stop them in some way? What was their reaction to this? Did you perhaps join in on one side or the other?

(h) '*Miss Healy wanted to join the other group*' (page 75)

Have you ever been in a situation where your loyalties have been divided between two people or groups of people, so that you have been uncertain which way to turn?

Have you, like Miss Healy, ever wanted to change sides in an argument, but been reluctant to do so for fear of hurting someone's feelings, or for some other reason?

(i) '. . . *arguing with her husband and daughter*' (page 75)

Has there ever been an occasion when you have been a member of a group which was having a difference of opinion with another group, when suddenly a more serious argument started between the members of your own group than existed in the first place?

Have you ever had a row with some other member of your family because they were embarrassing you by sticking up for you too vigorously?

Have you ever started an argument on some fairly small point but have then gone so far with it that you have been unable to drop it even though you would have liked to do so? Why could you not back out: because of the principle at stake, or on account of your personal pride, or because you were unwilling to admit that you were wrong?

(j) **Suggestions for writing:*

Tactless!

'Leave it to John!'

Worried

Getting Out of Trouble

The Row

Changing Sides

A Matter of Principle

'It's nothing to do with me!'

An Awkward Situation

Calming Someone Down

Nervous

9 Poems from 'Pomes Penyeach'

(a) '*A wonder wild*
In gentle eyes . . .' (page 77)

Can you recall the wonderment expressed by a very young brother or sister (or some other very small child you have known) at a particular object, like the flower in this poem? How do small children express their wonderment?

When you give a small child a present, what sort of pleasure do you get out of the action?

What do you like most about babies and other small children?

(b) '. . . *I wrap him warm*' (page 78)

Can you recall an occasion when one of your parents has been careful to protect you from something unpleasant? Have you ever resented being protected in this way?

Is it possible to over-protect a child? What happens when you *do* over-protect someone?

Have you ever felt the desire to protect someone else, perhaps even someone older than yourself, from something unpleasant?

Have you ever tried to protect someone else, but have only found that they wanted to be left alone to fend for themselves, and resented your attitude? How did you feel?

(c) *Suggestions for writing:*

'A wonder wild'

'Leave me alone'

Shelter

10 A Trip to Cork

(a) '*his father's property was going to be sold*' (page 79)

Can you remember a disaster of some sort overtaking your family or one of the members of it? In what way were you involved?

Has there ever been an occasion when there was some family problem which did not concern you directly so that you took little notice of it and did not share in the anxiety shown by the rest of the family? How did the other members of your family react towards you? Were they annoyed that you did not seem to have any interest in what was going on?

Have you ever been greatly disturbed or worried about your parents' problems without actually letting on to them that you were? Did you tell anyone about it?

(b) '*Stephen stood awkwardly behind the two men*' (page 81)

Have you ever felt out of place in adult company? What form did your discomfort take?

Have you ever been made deliberately to feel out of place by some other person?

Do you like the company of grown-ups, preferring it to that of your friends? When? Why?

(c) '*Mr Dedalus . . . searched the desks for his initials*' (page 81)

What is your attitude to elderly people trying to recapture the past in some way, perhaps, like Mr Dedalus, going over the old ground once again, perhaps by telling you about what it was like when they were your age? Do you sympathise with them or do you regard them as a nuisance?

Which moments of your own life, to date, do you think you will look back on with most pleasure when you are older?

(d) *'remember, whatever you do, to mix with gentlemen'* (page 83)

How do you regard the advice older people offer you? Have you ever been given a piece of advice by one of your parents or some other adult for which you have had cause later to be very grateful? Do you feel that adults spend too much time giving you advice, when you would rather find out things for yourself? Why do you think parents are so concerned with making sure that their children follow certain safe paths in life?

How do you feel when adults try to tell you what friends to have about you? Do you resent it when they advise you not to mix with certain people? Do you follow their advice?

What things do you most *want* advice on? To whom do you turn to get it?

(e) *'We were more like brothers than father and son'* (page 83)

Is your relationship with your parents a good one? Do you spend a good deal of time together? What sort of things do you do together? Can you recall a time when you have been especially happy in the company of your father and mother?

Do you feel that you can be absolutely frank with your parents? Is there any subject which you would prefer not to discuss with them?

Are your parents strict with you? Do you find it easy to live up to the standards they expect of you?

Would you say that your parents have very similar interests to yours? What are they?

Would you say that your parents are good friends to you?

(f) *'One humiliation had succeeded another'* (page 85)

Can you think of a time when *you* have felt humiliated by one thing after another? Whose fault was it?

What sort of thing humiliates you most? How do you avoid it? How do you cope with it when it happens?

Do you ever feel humiliated at school?

(g) *'I'm a better man than he is any day of the week'* (page 86)

Can you recall a time when one of your parents has

criticised you, saying that he or she was a better person than you when at your age?

What is your reaction when you are compared unfavourably with one of your friends, perhaps because he works harder or is better at some activity or other or behaves better at home or in public?

(h) '*Thanks be to God we lived so long and did so much good*' (page 87)

Do you think the older generation is complacent? How do you feel about the way older people tend to criticise the younger generation, because of their manners or their behaviour or because they want to go their own way and not follow the paths their parents have trodden?

Do you think youth has any duty towards age?

(i) **Suggestions for writing:*
Family Disaster
Out of Place
Looking Back
Unwanted Advice
My Family
The Old and the New
'Anything you can do I can do better'
The Future
Recapturing the Past
Going Our Own Way

On Our Own

11 After the Race

(a) '*Such a person . . . was well worth knowing*' (page 92)

Do you have any influential friends? Have you ever been introduced by your parents or friends to someone whom they thought might be of use to you in some way?

Have you ever tried to get an introduction to someone important because you needed their help or advice?

How would you behave if you were introduced to someone famous? Would it be in any way different from the way you behave towards any other stranger?

Do you have any friends at school who have considerable influence or power in the school? What is your attitude towards them? Perhaps you are an important person at school in this way – a prefect or captain, or a good sports-man? Do you think you have a greater responsibility in the way you behave and treat other people than you would have if you were not so influential?

(b) '*so does the possession of money*' (page 92)

What does having money in your pocket mean to you? Are you equally happy whether you are well off or not? What advantages do people with money have over the others at your school? Are you ever envious of how much money your friends have available?

Are you a generous person? Can you think of a time when one of your friends spent a lot of money on you? Did he ever expect you to do the same for him on another occasion? Have you ever treated someone you know and spent a lot of money on him or her? What satisfaction did you get out of doing so, if any?

(c) '*He had been seen*' (page 92)

Have you ever been glad to be seen by friends in the com-pany of some special person? Have you ever tried to arrange things so that you were seen by people you knew doing something impressive?

Do you like to be seen regularly in the company of a particular person?

(d) '*there was even a danger of personal spite*' (page 94)

Have you ever started a friendly discussion which suddenly got out of control and became deadly serious? Talk about it. What caused it to get out of hand?

Do you ever lose your temper when you do not intend to?

What sort of things do people say to each other when they lose their tempers?

Do they mean them?

(e) '*What merriment!*' (page 95)

Have you ever been a member of a group whose high spirits got out of hand so that its members started to do silly or irresponsible things which they would not have dreamed of doing in normal circumstances? Talk about it.

What sort of silly things do you do when you get into a very good mood with your friends?

What sort of things do adults do when they get into this sort of mood?

Have you ever been criticised for 'letting your hair down' in this way? By whom?

(f) '*He knew that he would regret in the morning*' (page 96)

Have you ever done something (and enjoyed it) which, all the time you were doing it, you knew you would regret later? What made you carry on in spite of the fact that you knew that you would regret it?

Do you have any habits which you know it would be better for you to give up, and over which you have a conscience, but which you still carry on because they give you pleasure?

(g) *Suggestions for writing:*

The Quarrel
Letting Our Hair Down
Regrets
Influence
Well-off!
Showing Off
A Useful Friend
The Game that Went Wrong

12 Poem: 'Ecce Puer'

(a) '*May love and mercy*
Unclose his eyes!' (page 97)

What wish would you have for your children? How would you wish life to treat them? Which of the benefits of life would you rate as most important for them? – love or mercy (like Joyce) or something else?

What do your parents chiefly hope for you and your generation? What qualities in your family life have your parents always tried to emphasise?

Is there anything that you would like your generation to leave for its children and other future generations? What sort of world do you wish to make for them?

(b) '*O, father forsaken,*
Forgive your son!' (page 97)

Is there any occasion in your past relationship with your parents which you are ashamed of and genuinely regret, wishing that it had never happened?

(c) *Suggestions for writing:*

A Wish for Future Generations
My Son
Regret
'I wish it had never happened'

13 Counterparts

(a) '*What is the meaning of this?*' (page 98)

Describe an occasion when you have been on the carpet for some misdeed.

Have you ever caused someone else to get into trouble? Did they deserve it? What happened?

Have you ever told off someone younger and weaker than yourself. How did they react? What manner did you adopt? Were you justified in telling them off in this way?

(b) '*He felt strong enough to clear out the whole office single-handed*' (page 101)

Can you recall an occasion when you have felt so frustrated and enraged that you thought the only way to get over it was to do something violent?

Do you ever feel like smashing things when you get into a temper? Have you ever actually done so?

How would you try to treat someone who was in such a state that he or she was behaving violently? Have you ever actually been in this situation?

(c) '*He had been obliged to offer an abject apology*' (page 102)

Have you ever been forced to apologise to someone for something you had done? Did you want to do so? What sort of mood were you in when you made the apology? Was it accepted?

Have you ever been forced to apologise for something which you had not done?

Have you ever refused to apologise to someone when asked to do so?

Have you ever demanded an apology from someone else for something they had done involving you? Why did you feel that you needed to have the apology? What was your attitude while the apology was being made? How did you behave towards the person afterwards?

(d) '*As he walked on he preconsidered the terms in which he would narrate the incident to the boys*' (page 103)

When you recount events that have happened to you, do you always tell the exact truth, or do you tend to distort them slightly to make a better story?

Do you know someone who always exaggerates in what he or she says?

(e) '*The trial began*' (page 106)

Have you ever been forced to play a game or take part in a

competition against your will? Did the fact that you were being forced to play alter your attitude to the game?

(f) '*He had lost his reputation*' (page 106)

How important is your reputation to you? What sort of reputation is it?

Have you ever had a reputation for being good at some sport or perhaps at some subject at school which you slowly lost over the years?

Is it better to lose your reputation slowly over the course of months or years or to lose it all at once?

Can you think of an occasion when you or some friend (perhaps an adult) lost a reputation because of an incident that occurred?

(g) '*You let the fire out!*' (page 107)

Have you ever been in such a bad temper with yourself that you have taken it out on other people? Have you ever hurt someone else because *you* had been hurt in completely different circumstances?

Have you ever been on the receiving end of a situation like this, perhaps when one of your parents or an older brother or sister has punished you because something had gone wrong for them at work?

(h) *Suggestions for writing:*

On the Carpet
Frustration
Making an Apology
A Lost Reputation
Unfair!
A Tall Story
Rage
Unwilling to Play
The Calm After the Storm

Further Reading

James Joyce

Those who wish to read more of the books from which this selection has been made will find the following editions useful:

Dubliners, Jonathan Cape, Chatto *Queen's Classics*, Triad Panther

A Portrait of the Artist as a Young Man, Jonathan Cape, Heinemann Educational, Triad Panther

Chamber Music, Jonathan Cape

These books, together with most of Joyce's poetry and some of his other writing, are also to be found in

The Essential James Joyce (edited by Harry Levin) Jonathan Cape, Triad Panther

Other writers

The following are just some of the fine studies of childhood and growing up which may interest those who have found the Joyce extracts interesting and rewarding:

FOURNIER, ALAIN. *Le Grand Meaulnes*, Penguin.

BARSTOW, STAN. *Joby*, Penguin.

BUHET, GIL. *The Honey Siege*, Penguin.

COLETTE. *Ripening Seed*, Penguin.

GARNER, ALAN. *The Owl Service*, Penguin.

The Red Shift, Collins.

GOLDING, WILLIAM. *Lord of the Flies*, Faber.

HARTLEY, L. P. *The Go-Between*, Penguin.

HUGHES, RICHARD. *A High Wind in Jamaica*, Chatto.

KNOWLES, J. *A Separate Peace*, Heinemann, *New Windmill*.

LEE, HARPER. *To Kill a Mockingbird*, Heinemann, *New Windmill*.

LEE, LAURIE. *Cider with Rosie*, Longman, *Imprint Books*.

MACKEN, WALTER. *Rain on the Wind*, Macmillan.

McCULLERS, CARSON. *The Member of the Wedding*, Heinemann, *New Windmill*.

NAUGHTON, BILL. *One Small Boy*, Longman, *Imprint Books*.

OWEN, HAROLD. *Journey from Obscurity*, OUP.

SPARK, MURIEL. *The Prime of Miss Jean Brodie*, Macmillan.

STEINBECK, JOHN. *The Red Pony*, Heinemann, *New Windmill*.

THOMAS, DYLAN. *Portrait of the Artist as a Young Dog*, Dent, *Aldine Paperback*.

TWAIN, MARK. *Huckleberry Finn*, Heinemann, *New Windmill*.

WATERHOUSE, KEITH. *Billy Liar*, Longman, *Heritage of Literature*.

There is a Happy Land, Longman, *Imprint Books*.